Witch Is When My Heart Broke

Chapter 1

When I arrived at the office, there was another woman behind the desk with Mrs V.

"Jill, this is Doreen Daggers—an old friend of mine."

"Nice to meet you, Doreen."

"You too, Jill. V often speaks of you."

"You're probably wondering what Doreen's doing here," Mrs V said.

"Well, yes. I was a little surprised to see someone behind the desk with you."

"I've done myself a mischief, dear. While I was putting my knitting trophies back on the shelf after I'd polished them, I slipped and twisted my arm. It's rather painful."

"Have you had it checked out at the hospital?"

"That's really not necessary. I wouldn't want to waste their time. There's nothing broken; it'll be fine in a couple of days. But I have to finish a consignment of scarves for the bowling club, and I promised they'd be ready by the end of the week. Doreen, who by the way, everyone calls Mrs D, has gallantly offered to step into the breach."

Mrs V, Mrs G and now Mrs D. Not at all confusing.

"I see. Is she going to knit them for you?"

"No, she's going to be my right arm. We thought if we sat side-by-side at the desk like this, I could hold one of the needles with my good arm, and Doreen could hold the other one."

"Right, so sort of synchronised knitting then?"

"Yes, I suppose you could call it that."

"Well, good luck. I'll leave you two to it."

***

It was late afternoon, and I was so bored that I was counting paperclips when the door opened, and Mrs V popped her head inside.

"Alison Shine is here to see you. She has an appointment."

"Ally Sunshine?" I chuckled at my own joke, but it was obviously lost on Mrs V. "Don't you see? Ally? Sunshine? Alison Shine?"

Mrs V gave me a sympathetic look. "I'll send her in, shall I?"

"Yes, please."

My comedic skills were wasted.

Alison Shine was in her late thirties, and had too many freckles for her own good. She'd called me less than an hour earlier; something about the disappearance of her sister.

"Alison Shine?"

"Please, call me Ally."

"Okay, Ally. What can I do for you today?"

"Like I said on the phone, it's my sister, Carly Baxter. She's gone missing." Alison pulled a battered photo out of her pocket. "This is her."

The smiling woman in the photo appeared to be wearing a red jumpsuit.

"When did she disappear?"

"It only happened a few hours ago."

"Are you sure she's actually missing? A few hours isn't very long."

"She disappeared off the end of a bungee cord."

Now, there was a sentence you didn't hear every day of

the week.

"Sorry, I don't understand."

"Carly and her husband, Gerry, run a bungee jumping company called 'Bouncers'."

"I see."

That explained the jumpsuit.

"Do you know the Wyre Valley?"

"Yes, I went there on a picnic with my sister and her kids last year."

"There's a large footbridge which Bouncers often use. Carly and Gerry were there earlier today with a few customers. Just like always, Carly jumped off the bridge first, to demonstrate how it was done. But when the cord bounced back, she wasn't on the end of it."

"She fell?"

"Yes, no. I don't know."

"I'm not following."

"There was no sign of her in the valley below. The riverbed is dry, so it's not as though she could have been washed away. She just disappeared."

"How is that possible?"

"That's what I'm hoping you can find out."

"Have the police been informed?"

"Yes. I called them as soon as Gerry told me that Carly had gone missing. That was just before I got in touch with you. They said that adults disappear all the time, and that they normally turn up again."

"But surely this is different? Did you explain the circumstances?"

"Of course. When I did, they said they'd look into it, but I don't have much faith in the local police, and I know you don't either. I read that article attributed to you in The

Bugle."

Was that article going to haunt me forever?

"Are you and your sister close?"

"Quite close, yes."

"How often do you see one another?"

"Not so often in recent years. We lead very different lives."

"How do you mean?"

"Carly has always been the adventurous one—a real go-getter. She married young, and now she has her own business. I still live in our parents' house with Dad. I've only ever been able to take on part-time work because I have to fit it around looking after him; he hasn't been well for a long time. I have to go with him on his hospital appointments. I'm probably going to lose my current job, at Moby car wash, if I have to have any more time off."

"What about your sister? Was she having any problems that you were aware of?"

"Her marriage isn't great. Gerry has had a number of affairs, but what really got her goat was when he had the audacity to accuse *her* of being unfaithful with Tony Bow."

"Who's that?"

"He owns a competing bungee jumping company."

"And is that likely?"

"Definitely not. Even though she despises Gerry, she would never cheat on him."

"What do you think has happened to her, Ally?"

She hesitated. "I think Gerry has done something to her, but I have no proof. That's what I want you to find out. Will you take the case?"

"Of course. I'll be happy to help."

"That's given me an idea," Winky said, after Ally had left. He was perched on the window sill.

I was almost afraid to ask. "What has?"

"Bungee jumping. I could set up a line from this window, and—"

"Don't even think about it."

"Has anyone ever told you that you're no fun at all?"

Out of courtesy, I called Jack Maxwell to let him know that I'd been hired to work on the Carly Baxter case.

"Bit of a weird one this, Jill."

"You're not kidding. Have your people been to the scene yet?"

"No. We want to speak to the husband first. When we can get hold of him that is."

"Hasn't he been in touch with you?"

"No. It was the sister who called it in, I believe."

"Don't you think it's strange that he didn't contact you?"

"Everything about this one is strange. I know that footbridge over the Wyre Valley, and one thing's for sure, if she did fall, it's a body we're looking for. No one could survive that drop."

I made my usual promise to keep him posted, and was about to hang up when he said,

"While I have you on the phone, I was just thinking about what your sister said that night at the policemen's ball."

"What was that?" As if I didn't already know.

"She mentioned that you still have all your dancing medals at your flat."

"She did say that, didn't she?" I was going to kill Kathy.

"I wondered if it would be possible for me to pop over to see them some time? You can talk me through how you won them all."

Pop over to see my medals? Wasn't it supposed to be etchings?

"That sounds great."

"Sometime soon, hopefully?"

"Soon? Yeah. Why not?"

***

I planned to start on the Carly Baxter case first thing the next morning unless she turned up in the meantime. That was still a strong possibility in my book. Tonight though, I was going to have a few choice words with that sister of mine.

Just when I'd thought I'd dug myself out of a hole over the ballroom dancing escapade, Kathy had dropped me right back into it. She'd told Jack Maxwell all about my so-called dancing medals — the ones I didn't have.

"To what do I owe this unexpected pleasure?" Kathy had a bag full of Lego in her hand when she opened the door.

"I've got a bone to pick with you."

"Obviously not your toe bone. That seems to have healed nicely." She laughed. "I really don't believe you, Jill. How on earth did you manage to persuade someone to put a plaster cast on your foot?"

"It was broken. A bus ran over it."

"Don't give me that load of old rubbish. You might be able to fool Jack Maxwell; he is only a policeman after all, but you can't fool me. You didn't break your toe. You faked it because it was the only way to get out of the competition."

"So, are you saying you don't believe your only sister?"

"That's exactly what I'm saying. In fact, I'd bet a million pounds that you didn't break your toe."

"I'm not here to discuss my toe. Like I said, I have a bone to pick with you."

"What have I done this time?"

"Aren't you going to invite me in? I could kill a cup of tea and a custard cream."

"You're in luck. I filled your Tupperware box only yesterday."

"Good thing, too."

Ten minutes later, we were in the living room. Kathy was bemoaning my exacting sugar requirements as usual, but at least she did have a box full of pristine, uncontaminated custard creams for my delectation.

I grabbed three biscuits.

"Hey, they've got to last, you know." She slammed the lid shut.

"I've only taken three."

"Yes, but I know you. First you'll have three, then another three, and the next thing you know, they'll all be gone."

"Never mind the custard creams. I'm not very pleased with you."

"What have I done this time?"

"You told Jack that I still have all my imaginary dancing medals."

"You were the one who told him you were an expert

ballroom dancer."

"Yes, but I'd wiggled my way out of that with my cunning plan."

"So you're admitting it then? The broken toe was a hoax?"

"Yes, all right, if you must know. I got a friend at the hospital to put a cast on my foot."

"I knew you were faking it."

"Anyway, I'd more or less dug myself out of that hole, and then you and Peter come along and tell Jack that I've still got all my medals, and suggest that he should come around and see them."

"That was pretty funny, wasn't it?" She laughed.

"*I* don't think so."

"I don't know what you're worried about, Jill. He's never going to take you up on it. He's probably forgotten already."

"Yeah, well, that's where you're wrong. Guess who I just spoke to on the phone."

"Really?" She laughed. "Oh dear."

"Yes, oh dear. He said that he'd really like to look at my medals, and have me talk him through how I won them all."

"That should be an interesting conversation. Can I sit in on it?"

"No, you can't. It's not as though I have any medals to show him. What am I supposed to do?"

"I'm going to give you the same advice as I gave you when you first told me about this ballroom dancing charade. Come clean! Tell him the truth. Say that you can't dance. That you've *never* been able to dance. Tell him you don't have any medals."

"Are you kidding? Is that the best you can come up with?"

"It's the only thing you *can* do."

"I can't. Not after everything I've already told him. And certainly not after pretending to break my toe."

"So, what are you going to do then?"

"There must be a way I can get my hands on some dancing medals. I could pretend they're mine, and make stuff up about them."

"You're going to make this even worse than it already is."

"Why? I can't see a problem with that plan."

"*That's* the problem. The fact that you can't see a problem. Look, if you're adamant that you want to go through with this lunatic plan of yours, I know where you can probably get your hands on lots of dancing medals."

"Where?"

"Lottie Baines."

"Spotty?"

"You're doing it again with the name calling!"

"Sorry. I didn't mean that. Has Lottie got medals for dancing?"

"Of course she has. Like I told you before, she and I used to dance all the time. When we didn't have you to hold us back, we were pretty good. Lottie went on to do all types of dancing including ballroom."

"I didn't know that."

"That's because you drifted away, and started to hang around with your nerd friends."

"My friends were not nerds."

"Anyway, Lottie won tons of medals and cups. I'm pretty sure she's still got them."

"Do you think she'd lend them to me?"

"She might. Unless she remembers what you used to call her."

"I didn't call her spotty to her face."

"That doesn't make it any better."

"I know. I was horrible back then, wasn't I?"

"Yes."

"You don't have to agree. Will you ask her for me?"

"No chance. I'm not doing your dirty work. If you want to borrow Lottie's medals, then you're going to have to eat humble pie, and ask her yourself."

"But if she remembers what I used to call her, she'll probably slam the door in my face."

"That's a chance you're going to have to take."

I had no choice. I didn't have money to spend on *new* medals, If I could borrow Lottie's, I could make up a story about how I'd won each of them. Hopefully, that would be an end to the whole sorry tale. I wondered how Lottie had turned out; she was probably a spinster.

What do you mean like me? I'm not a *spinster*. I'm *single*. Big difference.

Chapter 2

The next morning, when I arrived at the office, Mrs V and Mrs D were still knitting, side by side.

"Morning, Mrs V. Morning, Mrs D. How are the scarves coming along?"

"Very well. We seem to have improved our coordination, don't we, D?"

"Yes, V. It's working much better now."

"That's good to hear."

"Incidentally, Jill," Mrs V said. "I think there's something wrong with the lights in your office."

"How do you mean?"

"Look."

Sure enough, a white light was flashing on and off inside my office.

"Have you been in there, Mrs V?"

"No, we've been too busy with this knitting."

"Okay. I'd better go and see what's going on. Maybe it just needs a new bulb."

Once inside, I could see the problem. There, on the ceiling where the light should have been, was a rotating glitter ball. And then the music started.

"What the heck?"

The volume was unbearable; the bass beat felt like it was inside my head, and I could feel the floor vibrating beneath me.

"What's going on in there?" Mrs V yelled. "Are you all right, Jill?"

"Yeah, I'm okay."

Over where the sofa normally was, there was now a DJ console. And behind it stood Winky who was wearing shades and headphones. He was hard at work mixing tracks.

"Winky!" I shouted, but he was oblivious to my presence.

The music was getting louder and louder; it felt as though my eardrums were about to burst.

"Winky! What are you doing?"

He still couldn't hear me. I walked across the room, and banged my hand on the console, causing the stylus to jump off the records.

Winky pulled off his headphones. "Hey, mind the vinyl!"

"What's going on?"

"Isn't it obvious?"

"It looks like you've set up a disco."

"Very good. We'll make a P.I. of you yet."

"I know *what* you're doing. What I want to know is why you're doing it in my office?"

"The acoustics in here are superb."

"I don't care about the acoustics. You can't run a disco in here. This is my place of work."

"Don't worry, I won't be inviting anyone over. I'm just practising my set."

"Your *set*?"

"Come on, Jill. You're not that old. You must know what a *set* is."

"Yes, I know what a set is. But since when were you a DJ?"

"I've been a DJ since I was a kitten. But I've had so many other things going on in my life recently that I had to put it on a back burner. Then today, I got the urge to start gigging again."

"Gigging where?"

"Clubs of course."

"No club is going to employ a cat as a DJ."

"That's where you're wrong. There are any number of feline nightclubs who will be only too happy to give me a spot."

"There are *feline* nightclubs?"

"Of course there are! Where do you think cats go in the evening? I bet you think they go hunting for mice, don't you?"

"Well, yes, I suppose—"

"See that's just part of the whole masquerade. You humans are so easy to fool. Most cats are out clubbing. Then in the morning, they pick up a dead mouse from Dead Quick Mice, and drop it on the doormat when they get home."

"Dead Quick Mice?"

"A brilliant idea. I wish I'd come up with it. There's a whole chain of them now."

"And they provide dead mice for cats to take back home?"

"Precisely!"

"So you've worked the feline nightclub circuit before?"

"Yes, but it's a few years ago. I'm a little rusty, which is why I needed to practise my set. Once I'm back up to speed, I'll just make a few phone calls—and DJ Winky will be back in action."

"But what's with the glitter ball? Even I know that went out with disco?"

"For humans, maybe. The glitter ball is still going strong among the feline clubbers."

Who knew?

"That's all well and good, but how am I meant to get any work done with all that noise going on?"

"If you actually had any work, I could see how that might be a problem. But that's not something that happens very often, is it?"

Cheek!

"Listen to this." He cued up the record. "What do you think?"

Before I could object, he had his earphones on again, and began to mix a couple of tracks. I hated to admit it, but it was actually quite good. I couldn't help myself. The next thing I knew I was boogieing to the beat.

Then I heard the door open behind me. I turned around to find Jack Maxwell staring at me in disbelief. Fortunately, Winky had taken the hint and hidden behind the desk.

"Jill?" Maxwell looked more than a little confused.

"Hi, Jack. How are you?"

"I'm okay." He glanced over at the console, and then back at me. "Are you?"

"You're probably wondering about all this?"

"Yeah. Just a bit."

"I can explain." Probably.

"Could you turn the music down?" He had his hands over his ears.

Could I? It was a good question. There were a thousand buttons on the console, and I had no idea which controlled the volume, so I just lifted the stylus—scratching the vinyl in the process.

"Thanks." Jack appeared to be waiting for something by way of explanation.

"This belongs to a friend. I said he could store it here for a few days while he moves house."

"I see. And the glitter ball?"

"I thought I'd better check to make sure that it hadn't been broken in the move."

"I see your big toe has mended."

Oh bum!

"Yeah, it's much better, thanks." I wiggled my foot around.

"That's a remarkably quick recovery."

"I've always healed fast."

"Look, I only popped in to say hello while I was in the area. And to ask if you've managed to track down Gerry Baxter. He seems rather elusive."

"No, I haven't been able to contact him either. Would you like a drink while you're here?"

"No, it's okay. I have a meeting back at the station." He glanced at the DJ console.

"And, I can see you're busy as usual. Enjoy your disco dancing. Oh, and I'm looking forward to seeing your dancing medals."

"Yeah. Can't wait to show them to you."

After he'd left, Winky climbed back up onto the desk.

"Medals?" He laughed. "You don't have any dancing medals."

"I know. I'm in big trouble."

"Oh, and by the way." Winky lifted his shades. "You owe me for the two records you've ruined."

***

I was hoping to speak to some of the other people who

had been on the bridge when Carly Baxter disappeared. The obvious person to start with would have been her husband, but despite numerous phone calls, I still couldn't get hold of him. The only other witnesses were the customers who had paid to make a bungee jump.

Bouncers had a small unit on the Freeman Industrial Park, which was about seven miles from my office. Unsurprisingly, when I got there, the place was locked up. I made my way around to the back of the building where I spotted an open window. It was tiny, and certainly not large enough for a human to squeeze through, but a bit of magic goes a long way. I shrunk myself, and then began to levitate. It took all my focus because I was being buffeted back and forth by a stiff breeze. I eventually managed to make my way to the open window, and climbed inside. Once I had lowered myself to the floor, I reversed the 'shrink' spell.

The office was small and basic. I tried to access the solitary computer, but it was password protected, so I checked the filing cabinet, and for once I was in luck. Inside, was a thick manila folder marked 'Bookings'. The paperwork inside was in date order with the most recent on top. There had been eight people due to take part in the bungee jump when Carly Baxter disappeared. I took a photo of the sheet of paper with my phone. It contained the names, addresses and contact telephone numbers for all those who had booked to jump.

Back at my office, I began to work through the list of names. The first three calls I made rang out; the fourth went straight to voicemail. On the fifth, I struck lucky.

"Hello?" said a young woman.

"Is that Jean Cumberland?"

"Yes, who's this?"

"My name's Jill Gooder. I'm a private investigator. I've been hired by the sister of Carly Baxter."

"The bungee jump woman?"

"That's right. Her sister has asked me to try to find her. Would it be possible for me to meet up with you to ask a few questions?"

"I guess so, but I'm not in town at the moment. I'll be back tomorrow."

"Do you know Coffee Triangle?"

"Yes. I sometimes go there on gong day."

"Can we meet there tomorrow? Say two o' clock?"

"Sure, I'll see you there."

***

The twins practically fell over themselves to get to me when I walked into Cuppy C.

"Jill! We've got amazing news!" Amber screamed.

"Yeah. It's brilliant!" Pearl yelled.

"Steady on girls. Let's have a seat, and you can tell me all about it."

We found a quiet corner, and they eventually managed to calm down enough to tell me their news.

"We've been asked to be in the video for Trixie Day," Amber said, almost breathless.

"Who?"

"What do you mean, *who*?" Pearl said. "Trixie Day!"

"Yeah. Who's she?"

They both sighed. "You're absolutely hopeless, Jill. You're supposed to be a witch, but you don't know anything about sup pop music at all, do you?"

"Apparently not. So is she big?"

"She's the coolest pop star there is at the moment. She's had tons of hits. Her album's at the top of the Candlefield charts, and her singles are selling like hot cakes."

"What kind of music is she into?"

"It's hard to describe. I'll lend you one of her albums."

"Okay, thanks. But, how come she's asked you to appear in her video?"

"Apparently, her new single is going to be called Twins," Amber said. "She's been searching for ages to find young female twins about our age to appear in the video. She's had all of her people searching high and low. Anyway, the other day, one of the women who work for her P.R. company, a woman called, what was her name?" She looked to her sister.

Pearl thought about it for a moment. "Emier. Patty Emier."

"Yeah, that's it, Patty Emier. She just happened to pop into Cuppy C for a coffee, and she saw us behind the counter."

"What did she say to you?"

"Nothing—we didn't even know she'd been in the shop. She didn't introduce herself at the time. The first we heard of it was a couple of days later when she telephoned. Apparently, she'd taken our photo, and sent it to Trixie Day's manager. He showed it to Trixie Day, and she said we were exactly what she was looking for."

"Wow. So you're going to be in her pop video?"

"It's amazing, isn't it?" Amber could barely contain her excitement.

"When is all this going to happen? Are they going to

come to the shop to do the video?"

"We don't know when or where it will happen yet, Patty Emier is going to let us know."

"Will you get paid?"

"We don't care," Amber said. "We just want to be famous. Everybody in Candlefield will see the video. Cuppy C will be buzzing after that. People will probably want our autographs."

"Don't get ahead of yourselves, girls. It's only a pop video."

"Not just any old pop video," Pearl said. "It's Trixie Day's pop video."

"I'm very pleased for you both. It sounds really exciting."

Chapter 3

Kathy was right—I was a terrible person. I did used to call Lottie, Spotty Lottie. And, to be honest, it never even occurred to me that I was being horrible at the time. How would I have liked it if someone had called me spotty? I would have been really upset. I never actually said it to her face, but I suppose that makes it even worse.

Hopefully, Lottie had been blissfully unaware of my name calling. But what if she had known? What if she still held a grudge? Was I going to get my comeuppance? I was about to find out because Kathy had asked if I could borrow her dancing medals, and she'd said I could. Lottie had been rather surprised by the request, but I'd already primed Kathy to say that my friend's young daughter wasn't very enthusiastic about taking ballroom dancing lessons. The girl's mother thought that if she could see the medals, that would encourage her to go ahead with them. It had sounded far-fetched even to me, but apparently Lottie was happy to help. I'd tried to persuade Kathy to collect them for me, but she'd refused point-blank. She said that if I wanted to borrow them, I would have to do it myself.

She lived in one of the more upmarket areas of Washbridge. When I arrived, I was astounded. Her house was huge, modern and obviously very expensive. It was one of the nicest properties I'd ever seen in Washbridge. I couldn't help but wonder what sort of woman Lottie had become. She'd been a gangly, awkward kid.

I parked on the road outside her house, and walked up the long drive, which had perfectly manicured lawns on either side. When I rang the bell, a staggeringly beautiful woman answered the door.

"Jill?"

It was only when I heard her voice that I realised it was her. "Lottie?"

"Hi! It's so great to see you. It's been ages." She threw her arms around me and gave me a hug.

I couldn't believe my eyes. How could the woman standing in front of me be Lottie Baines? She certainly wasn't Spotty Lottie now. Her complexion was blemish-free, and put mine to shame. Her hair looked amazing. Her make-up was subtle, but effective, and she looked as though she worked out every day.

"Come in, Jill. I'm so happy to see you again."

It was like stepping into a show house. Lottie certainly had exquisite taste.

"Kathy said you'd like to borrow my dancing medals?"

"Yeah, please. If that's okay."

"Of course it is. You're lucky though because I've nearly thrown them out a thousand times. They're just gathering dust in the garage. I haven't looked at them for years. Kathy said you've got a friend whose daughter might be interested in ballroom dancing?"

"That's right. I thought seeing your medals might encourage her to take it up."

"That's a great idea. I'm only too pleased to help. Anyway, what are you doing these days? Are you still working at your dad's old place?"

"Yeah, I took over the business."

"So you're a detective?"

"I am."

"Wow. That must be really exciting."

"It can be. What about you? What do you do?"

"I have my own business now too. I opened one fitness centre, and then another, and another—I've got a whole chain of them now."

"Really? That's fantastic!"

"If you ever decide to join a fitness club, let me know and I'll do you a sweet deal."

"Thanks. It certainly looks like *you* work out."

"I can hardly turn up to my own health club looking like a couch potato. Dan and I train together."

"Dan?"

"My husband. We've been married for nine years now. He runs the business with me. Look." She pointed to a photo on the hall table. The man standing next to Lottie was some kind of Adonis. How had Spotty Lottie ended up with a man like that? She had the perfect husband, the perfect house, and her own business, which if this house was anything to go by, was making a ton of money.

Jealous? Who me? You bet I was.

"Would you like to stay for a drink, Jill? We can talk about old times. Do you remember when we used to dance—you, me and Kathy?"

How could I forget?

"You were pretty rubbish back then." She laughed.

That's when it all came back to me. Lottie and Kathy used to take the mickey out of me because I was useless at dancing. They used to point at me and laugh. Suddenly, I didn't feel quite so bad about my name calling.

"Sorry, I can't stay Lottie—I'm on a case."

"How exciting! I don't want to keep you from that. I'll go and grab the box of medals."

She disappeared for a few minutes, which gave me time

to take a quick look around the ground floor of the house. It was spectacular, and must have cost a small fortune.

A couple of minutes later, she came back with the box.

"There you go. It's a bit heavy. There are a lot of them."

"Thanks for this, Lottie. I shouldn't need them for very long."

"Keep them for as long as you like. They're only gathering dust. I hope your friend's daughter decides to go ahead with the ballroom dancing."

"Me too. Well, see you soon."

"Bye, Jill."

***

It was ridiculous. Absolutely ridiculous. I hadn't bothered calling in the supermarket in town because I expected to be able to pick up custard creams from the convenience store across the road from my block of flats. But, they didn't have any.

"We have plenty of jammy dodgers," the woman behind the counter offered.

"Jammy dodgers? Is that meant to be a joke?"

"They're very popular with our customers."

"Not with me, they're not. Don't get me wrong. I enjoy a jammy dodger, but please, do not compare them to custard creams. Surely there's enough shelf space to accommodate both."

"Normally there would be, but we're running a special offer on jammy dodgers at the moment, so we need the shelf space for them. At least until the offer ends."

"What am I meant to do?"

"Buy some jammy dodgers?"

I walked out in disgust. How dare they call themselves a *convenience* store?

The newsagent next door had recently changed hands. It had been closed for almost two weeks while the property was renovated, but had now reopened. I decided to check it out.

"Good evening." The man behind the counter was wearing a fedora, which while very dapper, felt a little out of place in a newsagent. "I'm the new owner, Jasper. Jasper James. Do you live around here?"

"Yes, in the flats across the road."

"And do you have a regular newspaper?"

"No, not really."

"What about a magazine? We have lots of them. You look like you might enjoy a knitting magazine or perhaps crochet?"

"Not me. That would be my secretary."

"Maybe you're a gardener, then?"

"Not that you'd notice."

"We have magazines for every interest. What sort of things are you into? I didn't catch your name."

"Jill Gooder."

"Well, Jill, I'm sure there must be a magazine here that would suit your interests. What do you do for a living?"

"I'm a private investigator."

"How jolly interesting. Well, you're in luck. We've just taken delivery of the latest issue of P.I. Monthly."

Who knew there was such a thing?

"Would you like to try a copy?"

"Why not?"

He wandered down the row of magazines, and came back clutching one. On the cover was a photo of a man holding a magnifying glass. How very stereotypical. Still, perhaps it would have some useful tips on marketing—I certainly needed some.

"Would you like to take out a subscription?"

"I'll see what I make of this one, first."

***

Thanks to my inconvenient convenience store, I had only two custard creams to last me all evening. That was unless I could be bothered to jump in the car and go to the supermarket. I was still debating whether or not to go when there was a knock at the door. If it was Kathy, I was determined she wasn't going to get her hands on my last two custard creams. So, before I answered the door, I hid them in the wardrobe.

It wasn't Kathy.

"Jack?"

"I'm sorry to drop in on you unannounced like this, but I was in the area, so I thought I'd just pop over on the off chance. If you're going out or if you've got company, I can leave."

Jack Maxwell calling on me, unannounced? Things were looking up.

"No, it's okay. Come in. Can I get you a coffee or tea? I'm out of custard creams, but I have chocolate digestives, if you'd like one?"

What? Who are you calling selfish?

"Chocolate digestives are fine by me. Look, I'll be honest with you, Jill. I hoped you might have time to show me your collection of dancing medals."

Oh bum! What was I supposed to do now? They were

still in the box that Lottie had given to me. I hadn't even had a chance to look through them.

"You do have them here, don't you? Kathy said you kept them in the flat."

"She did say that, didn't she? They're in a box somewhere, and they're probably very dusty. I haven't taken them out for ages. I'd like to clean them up before you see them."

"No need for that. I understand how difficult it must be to keep them all clean. Particularly when you have as many as you do. I thought maybe we could take a quick look at them. You could talk me through where and how you won them."

"That sounds great."

What was I supposed to do? Maybe I could just bluff my way through it. How difficult could it be?

"Okay, I'll go get them."

I fetched the box from the wardrobe, and put it on the coffee table. "There you go."

"Wow! I didn't realise you had so many. It's probably just as well you weren't able to take part in the competition; you would have made me look like a complete amateur."

He pulled open the box, grabbed the first medal, and looked a little puzzled. When he picked out the next one, he looked even more confused. He took out two or three more, and put them all on the coffee table.

"I don't understand. Why do they all say Lottie Baines on them?"

Oh no! It had never occurred to me that they'd have her name engraved on them.

"Lottie Baines? Err — that's my stage name."

"Stage name?"

"Yeah. Mum and Dad didn't like to have mine and Kathy's names all over the papers, so they said we should use stage names when we went dancing. I chose Lottie Baines."

"What was Kathy's stage name?"

"Kathy's? Err — Anastasia — err — Belgrave."

"Anastasia Belgrave?"

"Yeah."

"And did Kathy win many medals?"

"None. She has two left feet."

"It's probably just as well. I'm not sure they would have been big enough to accommodate her name."

I somehow managed a smile.

Jack went through every medal, and asked me if I could remember the competition where I'd won it. Luckily for me, I have a vivid imagination, so I was able to make up all kinds of rubbish. Like the time I'd just managed to beat the local favourite to win the paso doble, and how I tied for first place in the foxtrot at Llandudno.

If I'd had any sense, I would have come clean and told him the truth, but the time for that was long gone. I should have been honest with him when he first asked me to be his partner, or at least on the day of the policemen's ball. There was no way I could do it now. Anyway, he seemed satisfied with my fairy stories.

When he'd been through them all, he said, "One thing's for sure, Jill. When you and I enter the next competition, we can't fail to win."

"Are there likely to be many more?"

"Lots of them. I'll let you know when the next one is."

"Great. Thanks."

Chapter 4

If Jean Cumberland had been hoping to hammer on a gong, she was out of luck because it was triangle day. Just the thought of a triangle made me shudder; I'd always had an irrational fear of them.

As soon as I stepped inside the coffee shop, I spotted a young woman, sitting alone, playing a triangle.

"Jean?"

"Jill? Sorry, I was miles away. The triangle reminds me of my school days."

"Mine, too. Not good memories though." I took the seat opposite her.

"I'm not sure there's much I can tell you about the woman who disappeared, but I'm happy to answer your questions."

"Thanks. Was it your first bungee jump?"

"It would have been. I was absolutely terrified. It wasn't even my idea. My stupid sister signed us up for it, and only told me after she'd done it."

"My sister's a bit like that too, but at least Kathy hasn't signed me up for bungee jumping yet."

"When we arrived at the bridge, I was scared to death. I was literally shaking. Sharron, that's my sister, said I had to go through with it because she'd already paid. I would have gladly paid her back double not to have to jump, but she wasn't having any of it. As it turned out, it didn't matter."

"Can you talk me through what happened?"

"There were two of them running the show: a man and a woman. I think they were man and wife. Anyway, the man checked that our harnesses were fastened correctly, got us to remove our jewellery, and gave us each a bag to put our possessions in. Then, he told us to go over to the side of the bridge. The woman instructor was already sitting astride the railings."

"Did the man stay with you?"

"No. Once he'd checked our harnesses, he went back to the transit van which was parked on the road. He locked our possessions in it."

"And the woman?"

"She was supposed to jump off the bridge so that we could see exactly what was involved. Then it would be our turn."

"Did the man check *her* harness?"

"No. He only checked ours. I assumed she knew what she was doing."

"Then what happened?"

"She said, *'Watch me, because in a few minutes you'll be doing this. Three, two, one.'*

Then she threw herself backwards off the bridge. None of us moved; we just stood there open-mouthed. The man came back over to us just as the cord came flying back up. She wasn't on it. Somebody screamed, and I said to Sharron, *'She must be dead.'*

We all looked down into the valley. I expected to see her lying on the rocks, but there was no sign of a body. The man rushed off the bridge, and started to make his way down the hillside. We followed because we didn't really know what else to do. Then, when we got to the valley floor, we all searched for the woman. I thought for sure we'd find her body, but there was no trace of her."

"How did her husband seem?"

"That was the funny thing. He wasn't as upset as I

would have expected. Maybe it was just the shock."

***

I'd asked Mrs V to check what was left of the Yellow Pages to find the name of the competing bungee jumping company that Tony Bow owned.

"It's called 'Jump To It'."

"Jump Twit? Are you sure about that? That's a very strange name."

"Of course I'm sure. Look!" She pointed to a large ad on the page under the heading of 'Bungee Jumping'.

"Ah! 'Jump To It'."

"That's what I said."

I called the number, and a young woman answered, "Jump To It. How can I help you?"

"Is that the company which Tony Bow owns?"

"Yes, that's right."

"Can I have a word with him?"

"He's not in at the moment. He's taking a class."

"It's rather important that I speak to him."

"I can give him a message."

"Is there any chance you could tell me where I could find him? It's rather urgent that I speak to him today."

"He's out at Greenland Valley. Do you know the footbridge there?"

"Yeah, I know the one. What time is he likely to be finished with the class?"

"About two o' clock. He told me he'd call in then to see if there were any enquiries he needed to respond to."

"So, if I got there around two, I might catch him?"

"You can try, but I can't promise."

I parked in the car park at one end of the footbridge that spanned the Greenland Valley. There were three other vehicles there, including a van with the name 'Jump To It' on the side. As there was only one person on the bridge, I assumed the class must have finished.

"Are you Tony Bow?"

"Yeah, that's me."

"Your office said I'd find you here."

"If you want to make a booking, you'll need to do it through the office because they've got my diary."

"It isn't about a booking. My name is Jill Gooder. I'm a private investigator."

He stopped what he was doing and stared at me. "Is it about Carly Baxter?"

"You've heard about it?"

"Of course. I saw it in the paper. It was only a matter of time until something like this happened."

"What do you mean?"

"Until someone was killed."

"What makes you think Carly is dead? She's only missing."

"If she fell off the footbridge over Wyre Valley, she's dead. You can trust me on that one."

"What did you mean when you said it was only a matter of time?"

"Gerry Baxter's always been all about the money. He undercuts me at every turn. But he can only do it because he takes shortcuts. His attention to safety is not what it should be."

"Have you lost much business to him?"

"He's definitely taken some customers with his silly

prices, but I still do okay. And, at least I can sleep at night. I know my customers aren't risking life and limb when they bungee jump with me. I wouldn't want any of my family or friends jumping with him."

"Do you have any idea how she could have just disappeared like that?"

"None. It's impossible. Either you're on the cord or you're not. If you're not, then you're plunging to your death. Something doesn't smell right about this."

"How'd you mean?"

"I wouldn't trust Gerry Baxter as far as I could throw him. If I were you, I'd start by asking him where his wife's body is."

"How well do you know Carly?"

"We met from time to time. She seemed nice enough."

"That's all?"

"What else?"

"Apparently, her husband accused her of having an affair with you."

He laughed. "That's the most ridiculous thing I've ever heard."

"So it's not true?"

"Of course it isn't. That husband of hers is a complete idiot."

"Okay. Thanks for your time, Mr Bow."

"No problem."

Either he was telling the truth or he was a very good liar.

***

My door was ajar, and I could hear voices in the outer office. I recognised them immediately; it was Mr and Mrs

Pride—Gertie's parents. My heart sank. I had a horrible feeling I knew why they were here. Since Gertie had moved to Washbridge, she'd landed herself in a lot of trouble by using magic at other people's expense. And she'd apparently told her parents that it was all my idea.

"Mr and Mrs Pride are here," Mrs V said.

I considered saying I was too busy to see them, but it would only be putting off the inevitable.

"Send them in, Mrs V."

They greeted me like a long lost friend; that was encouraging, at least.

"Nice to see you again, Jill," Mr Pride said. "How are you keeping? How's the dart playing?"

"I don't play much these days." Out of the corner of my eye, I saw Winky rolling around on the sofa in hysterics. Thankfully, the Prides didn't seem to notice. "Have a seat. Would you like a drink?"

"No, we're okay," Mr Pride said. "Look, you know we'll always be grateful to you for finding Gertie for us."

I sensed a 'but' coming.

"But—"

See! What did I tell you?

Mrs Pride stepped in. "Look, Jill. Gertie tells us that you've encouraged her to use magic in Washbridge. To play tricks on people—just for a laugh."

Oh, boy.

"That's not really true. When I first met Gertie, she was totally against moving to the human world. She was particularly worried she wouldn't be able to use magic in Washbridge. I wanted her to realise that she didn't have to give up her magic, but I did say that she'd have to be careful not to let humans see what she was doing."

"I thought it was probably something like that," Mrs Pride said. "I think Gertie only listened to half of what you said."

Her husband nodded. "Have you heard what she's been up to?"

I wasn't sure whether the Prides knew that Gertie had already been to see me, but there was no point in trying to hide it now.

"She did actually call in a little while ago with her two friends, Holly and Juniper. She told me that they'd been playing tricks on people using magic, and that she'd been in trouble at school."

"The school isn't very happy with her at all," Mr Pride said. "We've been called in a couple of times now. She's using magic to mess about and play tricks on the teachers. Fortunately, no one's worked out what she's doing yet, but she's not going to get away with it forever. We're really worried. Sooner or later she's going to overstep the mark, and someone back in Candlefield will hear about it."

"When she came to see me, I told her that the Rogue Retrievers were on the lookout for sups who were abusing their magical powers in the human world. I thought that might shake her up a little, and make her think again."

"I can't say we've noticed much difference in her behaviour," Mr Pride said. "We were called in only yesterday by the headmaster. Gertie had apparently upset one of the other children."

"Doing what?"

"We don't know the precise details, but apparently one of the other girls had said something nasty to Gertie. Shortly afterwards, the same girl came running out of the toilet, screaming her head off. Gertie had cast a spell which made the poor girl see a pig's head when she checked the mirror. Gertie reversed the spell as soon as the girl came back into the classroom, but the damage was already done. The teacher didn't know exactly what had happened, but he was pretty sure Gertie was behind it. Which of course she was.

The headmaster called us in, and said that we needed to have a word with Gertie and sort it out because wherever she went, trouble seemed to follow. We sat Gertie down last night, and had a long chat with her. She said she was sorry, but she didn't really look it. I have a horrible feeling that it's going to carry on. If they throw her out of school, I don't know what we'll do. We might not get her into another school in Washbridge, and what happens then? If we have to move back to Candlefield, I'll be out of a job." Mr Pride sighed. "I'm not sure if there's anything you can do, Jill, but we thought we'd come to see you just in case."

"I think I know a way to stop her bad behaviour."

"What exactly did you have in mind?"

"I'd rather not say. It's nothing nasty or horrible, but hopefully it will have the desired effect. What do you think? Will you trust me to do this?"

They both nodded.

Chapter 5

The next morning, I heard something being pushed through the letterbox, and found a leaflet lying on the mat. I assumed it was yet more advertising rubbish. When I picked it up, I realised it was actually an invitation with my name handwritten on the top. I opened the door to see who had delivered it, but the corridor was empty.

The leaflet was headed Z-Watch. I had a quick skim through it, but there was very little detail. It seemed to be some kind of Neighbourhood Watch scheme. But why call it Z-Watch? Then, the penny dropped. I lived on the Zander estate; Z for Zander. They were probably leafleting people to see if they could attract new recruits.

When I set off for work, I found Luther, Mr Ivers, and Betty all in the front entrance, chatting.

"Hey, guys. Have you all received an invitation to join the local Neighbourhood Watch?"

Mr Ivers shook his head.

"I didn't." Betty shrugged.

"I haven't received anything either," Luther said. "When did you get it?"

"Just now. I assumed they were contacting everyone to try and find new recruits."

"Perhaps they targeted you because you're a private investigator," Luther said. "They probably thought you would be ideally suited."

"That could be it, I suppose."

"You should join," Mr Ivers said.

"Yeah," Betty agreed. "You should definitely join. The crime rates around here are soaring."

That was rich coming from our resident shoplifter.

"I agree," Luther said. "I'd feel a lot safer knowing that people like you are watching the neighbourhood for us."

My phone rang.

"I'm just on my way out, Kathy."

"I only called for a quick chat. How's things?"

"Okay. I just got invited to join the Neighbourhood Watch."

"You should do it, Jill."

"I'm busy enough already."

"I would have thought if anyone had the time, it would be you. Pete and I are in our Neighbourhood Watch."

"I don't remember you mentioning it."

"It's no big deal. We meet about once a month for an hour or so to discuss any problems anyone is aware of. Generally, though, it's just a question of keeping a lookout to make sure there are no suspicious characters about— other than you of course."

"You're so funny."

"I do my best."

"So, do you think I should check it out?"

"Why not? It's not like you're forced to sign up. Just go along and hear what they have to say."

"I might do that. Anyway, I'd better get going. I have important things to do."

"Of course you do. Okay, catch you later."

If Kathy could hold down a job, look after two kids, run the house, and still find time for Neighbourhood Watch, I didn't have any excuse not to do it. Maybe I'd give it a try. I might even meet some hot guys there.

But right now, I had an important phone call to make.

When I arrived at Cuppy C, the twins were just on their way out.

"Where are you off to, girls?"

"We just had a call."

"*The* call," Amber said.

"*The* call?"

"From Trixie Day's people."

"Oh? Right. *The* call. So, are you going to shoot the pop video now?"

"Yeah."

"You do realise it's raining, don't you?"

They were both wearing summer dresses, and neither of them was wearing a coat. "You're going to get absolutely soaked."

"Patty said that we had to wear these, and that we had to get to the park straight away. We're going to get a taxi."

"Why would they want you to wear summer dresses when it's pouring with rain?"

"Patty said they can use special effects to make it look as though it's a sunny day, even though it's raining."

"That's really clever."

"I know," Amber said. "It's fantastic what they can do these days."

"Couldn't you at least take an umbrella?"

"We don't need to because the taxi will be here in a minute. Patty said they'll meet us in the park, near the lake, and there'll be plenty of shelter. So, we'll be okay."

"Don't catch your death of cold."

"We'll be fine."

Yeah, I don't think so. Snigger.

I treated myself to a strawberry cupcake and a latte while I waited. Just over an hour later, the twins were back. They were absolutely soaking wet, and looked thoroughly miserable.

"Girls, whatever happened?" I should get an Oscar.

They dripped their way across the room to join me at the table.

"Nobody was there." Amber looked dejected.

"The park was empty," Pearl said. "We waited for ages next to the lake, just like Patty told us, but nobody turned up. We're absolutely soaked through. I'm frozen."

"Oh dear. Tell me something, girls. The woman who rang you earlier to tell you to go to the park—did she sound anything like this?

Hi, it's Patty Emier. We need you in the park straight away—next to the lake. Wear summer dresses. We can use special effects to make the weather look sunny. We'll provide umbrellas and there'll be plenty of shelter."

The twins stared at me in disbelief.

"That was you?"

I laughed. "Yeah. It was me."

"You're Patty Emier?"

"None other."

"You made the whole thing up?"

"Pretty much. Hilarious, isn't it?"

"No, it isn't," Pearl said. "Why would you do that?"

"Well, I'll give you a clue." I took a notepad and pen from my handbag. "What was Patty's last name?"

"Emier," Pearl said.

"And who was the video for?"

"Trixie Day," Amber said.

"Now let's see what we've got. Patty worked in *PR*. Her last name is *EMIER*. And she wanted you to appear in a video for *Trixie DAY*."

I pushed the note in front of them.

"What do we have here? Oh, yeah. PREMIER DAY. The day when you faked flu so you could go shopping. You must remember that, don't you?"

If looks could kill, I would have been dead on the spot.

Revenge was so very sweet!

***

When I'd asked to see Daze, she'd suggested we meet in the park. We'd arranged to see each other on the bench at the top of the park, near to the entrance which Barry and I usually used. Luckily for me, the rain had stopped, and the sun had fought its way through the clouds.

I was running a little early.

Daze was there already, but she wasn't alone. She was locked in a passionate kiss with someone who I assumed was her new boyfriend, Haze. I felt a little awkward. She obviously hadn't expected me to arrive early. As I got closer, Daze spotted me, and they pulled apart.

"Hi, Jill," Daze said, looking more flustered than I'd ever seen her. She was usually cool, calm and collected, but today she was actually blushing.

"I'm a bit early, I hope that's okay."

"No problem. This is Haze. Haze, this is Jill Gooder."

He was a mountain of a man. Six-feet-five if he was an inch, and built like the proverbial.

"Hello, Jill." His voice didn't match his build. It was

rather high-pitched, but he had a lovely smile.

"Hi, nice to meet you, Haze."

"You too. Daze has told me a lot about you. Anyway, I know you two have business to discuss, so I won't hang around."

He gave Daze a quick peck on the cheek, and then went on his way.

"Have a seat, Jill," Daze said. "Sorry about that. I thought Haze would be gone before you arrived."

"No problem. It was nice to meet him. How are you two getting on?"

"Famously." She had a broad smile on her face. "I think he might be the one."

"Really? So soon?"

"Yeah, sometimes you just know, don't you?"

As if I'd know.

"Anyway," she said. "What is it you wanted to see me about?"

"I need a favour."

"Go on."

"Do you remember when you and Blaze followed those two girls for me in Candlefield?"

"You mean the girl who had supposedly disappeared?"

"That's the one."

"She hasn't gone missing again has she?"

"No, nothing like that. She was a bit worried about moving to the human world, so I gave her a sort of pep talk. I said she'd still be able to use magic, but that she would have to be discreet. It appears that she misinterpreted what I said because she's gone a bit wild, and is now running amok with her magic. She's disrupting her lessons in school, and having a lot of fun at the expense of humans. I had a word with her, and I thought that had done the trick, but it obviously didn't because her parents came to see me, and they're still very worried about her behaviour. They asked if there was anything I could do, and I thought of you."

"Do you want to scare her a little?"

"That's the general idea."

I spent the next ten minutes explaining to Daze what I had in mind; she seemed quite happy to go along with the plan. I was just about to leave when I noticed a young couple walking towards us. I turned to Daze.

"Is that who I think it is?"

Daze nodded.

It was Blaze, arm in arm with a young woman who was also dressed in a catsuit. They were of a very similar height and build, and looked very relaxed in each other's company.

"Hiya, Jill," Blaze said. "This is my girlfriend, Maze, short for Maisie."

"Right. So, Blaze and Maze?"

"Oh, yeah." He grinned. "I never thought of that."

Maze laughed too; she seemed sweet but a little shy.

"Are you a Rogue Retriever too, Maze?"

"I'm an apprentice. I'm actually Haze's new partner."

"So is that how you and Blaze met?"

"That's right. We were lucky that Daze and Haze got together."

No wonder Blaze had been so keen to play cupid to Daze and Haze. He'd obviously done it so he could get close to Maze.

The crafty little so-and-so.

Chapter 6

There was still no word on Carly Baxter, so I decided to take a look at the Wyre Valley where she'd disappeared. The footbridge wasn't as high as the one on which I'd met Tony Bow. Even so, anyone falling from there definitely wouldn't have got up and walked away. And yet, it appeared that Carly Baxter had done just that.

I parked as close as I could get to the footbridge, and then walked towards its centre. My knuckles were white as I held on tight to the rail, and peered over the edge. It was a *very* long way down. Why anyone would want to fasten themselves to a rubber band, and then jump over the edge, was beyond my comprehension. And, to think they actually paid for the privilege!

There are some very crazy people around — and I should know!

I carried on to the far side of the bridge, and began to make my way down the hillside. Although it was a long drop to the bottom, the sides of the valley weren't particularly steep, so I was able to scramble down without too much difficulty.

There was no doubt in my mind; Carly Baxter could not have survived a fall from the footbridge. The area immediately below it was all rocks. I scrambled around for a little over thirty minutes — looking for what, I wasn't sure. Exhausted, I sat on a rock and looked up at the footbridge.

That's when I spotted it. There was a small patch of red which stood out against the grey metalwork of the underside of the bridge.

I was much too tired to climb back up the way I'd come,

so I took the lazy way.

Levitation took a long time, but I wasn't in any hurry. When I was level with the underside of the bridge, I pulled myself up onto one of the beams. There, snagged to the metalwork, was a small piece of red cloth – the same colour as the jumpsuit Carly Baxter had been wearing in the photo that Alison Shine had shown to me. How could it have got there? I looked all around, and eventually spotted a small ring clamp which had been screwed into the underside of the footbridge, directly above my head.

For the first time, things began to make sense. Carly Baxter must have been attached to the footbridge, by not one, but two bungee cords. When she jumped, she must have released the first cord, and allowed the second cord to pull her back up under the bridge.

When the people on the footbridge had looked down, they hadn't seen her because she'd been perched where I was now. I would probably never have worked it out if the cloth, which must have come from her jumpsuit, hadn't got snagged on the metalwork.

That still left a couple of questions: Why had she done it? And where was she now?

When I called Jack Maxwell to tell him that I had new information, he was just about to interview Gerry Baxter. He agreed to postpone the interview until I got to the police station, and brought him up to speed.

"What exactly are you suggesting, Jill?" Maxwell had his impatient head on when I arrived at the police station.

"I've told you, it was obviously some kind of trick. Carly Baxter was attached to two cords. She released the one that everyone saw come back empty. The second one took her back up under the bridge. While everyone was looking for her down on the valley floor, she must have made her way out along the underside of the bridge, and got away."

"So, where is she now?"

"I have no idea."

"Look, I'm going to interview Baxter. You wait out here, and I'll let you know what happens."

"Okay."

He left me outside the interview room, so I used the 'listen' spell to overhear what was being said. Maxwell and his assistant first went through the formalities of introducing themselves for the benefit of the tape, then they asked Gerry Baxter to do the same.

"Why am I here?" he said, obviously annoyed.

"We're trying to find your wife, Mr Baxter. I'm sure you want to help us to do that."

"Of course I want to find her, but I don't know what good asking me questions is going to do. You should be out there looking for her."

"All in good time. First though, I have a few questions that I need you to answer. Can you tell me why your wife had two bungee cords attached to her when she jumped?"

Baxter fell silent, and I could almost sense his discomfort through the wall.

"It — err." He stuttered. Maxwell had obviously caught him off guard.

"Are you denying that she had two cords attached to her?" Maxwell pressed.

"No."

"Was this whole thing some kind of stunt? You'd better tell us everything you know. It'll make it easier for you in the long run."

"Okay. Yes, it was. We thought that the press would get hold of it, and we'd get the headlines. You know what they say: there's no such thing as bad publicity."

"Don't you think you've carried this a little too far? Wasting police time is not a sensible thing to do. And it's something for which you'll be charged."

"I didn't call you; I just called the press. We never intended that the police should get involved. As soon as the article was published, Carly was going to re-appear, and that would have been the end of it. We thought the publicity might land us more business."

"So where is your wife now?"

"I don't know. Honestly. The plan was for us to meet in Black Woods after I'd fed the story to the press. But she didn't turn up. The last I saw of her was when she jumped off the bridge."

"And you haven't seen or heard from her since then?"

"Not a word."

"Do you seriously expect me to believe that, Mr Baxter?"

"It's the truth. I'm really worried about her."

Jack Maxwell kept at Gerry Baxter for almost an hour, but got no more out of him. When Maxwell came out, he and I went back to his office. For a moment, I almost forgot myself, and asked him whether he believed what Baxter had told him. That would have been embarrassing because, as far as Maxwell was concerned, I didn't know what had been said in the interview. I had to play dumb.

"How did it go?"

"It was all a publicity stunt, apparently. The idea was that they'd get it in the papers, then Carly Baxter would turn up out of the blue. He insists they never intended to involve the police."

"That's just stupid. Why would a story like that bring them more custom? I would have thought it would put people off."

"Who knows? People's stupidity no longer surprises me."

"Is he still insisting he doesn't know where she is?"

"That's exactly what he's saying. And, to be honest, I believe him. He seems genuinely worried."

"Why didn't she turn up after the papers had got hold of the story?"

"I have absolutely no idea, and until I do, I have no reason to hold Baxter any longer."

***

I had the radio on while driving back to the flat. The breaking news was that a woman's body had been discovered on the Freeman Industrial Park. The details were sketchy, and it could have been anyone, but I had a bad feeling about it.

There was a police cordon around the industrial unit which housed Bouncers, so I parked as near as I dared, and made myself invisible. Once through the cordon, I got as close as I could to where the body was still lying. It was Carly Baxter; I recognised her from the photo that her sister had shown to me.

There were several policemen on the scene, as well as a pathologist in white coveralls.

"What can you tell us?" One of the police officers addressed the question to the pathologist.

"There's no sign of a struggle. She was stabbed in the back. Either the assailant crept up on her or she knew and trusted him enough to stand with her back to him."

I was sure the discovery of the body would mean that Maxwell would be able to charge Gerry Baxter, but then the pathologist continued. "This happened within the last hour or so."

"Are you sure about that?" the police officer said.

"Absolutely."

Bum! If it had happened within the last hour or so, it couldn't have been Baxter. He'd been at the police station. So who *had* killed Carly Baxter?

***

I went straight over to Alison Shine's house, but there was no one in. I was just about to leave when her car pulled into the driveway. She looked surprised to see me and a little flustered. Perhaps she'd heard the news item on the radio and put two and two together.

"Have you found Carly?" she said.

Obviously she hadn't heard. This wasn't going to be easy.

"Shall we go inside?"

"What's happened, Jill?"

"Let's go inside, and I'll tell you."

She led the way into the living room.

"Well? What is it?"

"I'm sorry to be the bearer of bad news."

"No!" She screamed, and collapsed onto the sofa. "No! Not Carly! Are you sure? The police haven't contacted me."

"They will. Any time now."

"Was she — murdered?"

"I'm afraid so."

"Gerry did it! That man is evil. They should lock him up and throw away the key."

"It can't have been Gerry, Ally."

"Of course it was him. Who else would it be? I told you, didn't I? I told you he'd done this. I hate that man."

"It definitely wasn't Gerry."

"How can you be so sure?"

"Because at the time that Carly was murdered, Gerry was in police custody. I saw him there. Carly was still alive until a few hours ago."

Alison looked shocked. "I don't understand. Who else would want to kill her?"

"What about Tony Bow?" I suggested. "You said that Gerry suspected Carly of having an affair with him."

"She swore to me it wasn't true."

"But you did say that she and Gerry didn't have a happy marriage?"

"They didn't. Gerry is a horrible man. Maybe she did seek comfort with Tony. I don't suppose she told me everything."

"I think I should pay Tony Bow another visit."

"Will you let me know if you find anything?"

"Of course. Can I call someone to come and stay with you?"

"No. I'll be okay. It's not like anyone cares anyway."

Chapter 7

The next morning when I stepped out of my flat, Luther was in the corridor. I'd already made a fool of myself too many times with him, and I'd made a pact with myself not to do it again. From now on, I was going to play it cool.

"Morning," I said, as cool as you like.

"Good morning, young lady. And how are you on this beautiful day?"

He put his hand on my shoulder; he'd never done that before. What was going on?

"It does my heart good to see someone as pretty as you at this time in the morning," he said. "You've set me up for the day."

Wow. I was speechless. Although Luther was always friendly, he was never flirtatious. But there was no other word for it; he was definitely flirting with me. Steady on, Jill. Don't get carried away. Remember what you promised yourself; act cool.

"It's Jill, isn't it?" he said.

"Err, yeah." Strange question.

"You must call me Lou."

Lou? He wanted me to call him Lou? That must be the name he reserved for his closest friends.

"Okay, Lou."

"I wonder, Jill," he said, his hand still on my shoulder. "Would you be free for dinner tomorrow night?"

He'd asked me out for dinner once before, but when I'd arrived at the restaurant, there'd been a table full of guests. I wasn't going through that ordeal again.

"When you say dinner, Lou, do you mean a party of

people?"

"No. Just you and me. An intimate dinner for two."

Intimate? That was more like it! "Just the two of us?"

"Would you like that?"

"Yes, that would be very nice."

"Give me your number, and I'll call you later today to arrange a time and a place. How's that sound?"

"Fabulous."

At long last, a date with Luther! And, this time there could be no mistake.

***

It was time for me to put Gertie straight. Or at least to try. I'd shrunk myself, and was hiding near to the school bus stop. When she showed up, still half asleep, she dropped her backpack onto the ground close to me. When I was sure no one was looking, I jumped onto it, and slipped inside through the narrow gap under the flap.

Oh wow! I hadn't anticipated just how bad it would smell in there. Presumably, she used the same bag for her sweaty sports kit. It was pretty horrible, but there was no going back now. I lodged myself in a small area between her lunch box and pencil case, and then waited.

Suddenly I found myself falling backwards. Gertie had obviously picked up the bag and thrown it over her shoulder. I managed to scramble to my feet, and grabbed hold of the side of the lunch box to steady myself. When we got onto the school bus, she dropped the bag onto the floor with a thump. I was beginning to think this wasn't such a good idea after all. The same thing happened again when she got off the bus. By the time we got into the classroom, I was feeling quite disorientated. Hopefully now she'd stay put for a while.

When I peeped under the flap, I could see that Gertie and her friends had congregated at one side of the classroom. A few minutes later, the door banged open, and in walked a middle-aged man with short brown hair, and a very serious expression.

"Right. To your desks, please," the teacher said. "We don't have time to waste; we have a lot of ground to cover this morning."

Everyone took their seats.

"Today, we're going to be talking about medieval Britain."

A general groan went around the room. The teacher turned to face the blackboard, and as he began to write, I noticed something drifting across the room, very close to the ceiling. It was a rain cloud.

Moments later, rain began to pour down onto the teacher's head. The poor man looked shocked, and rushed over to the door. Before he could turn around to see what had happened, Gertie had reversed the spell and the cloud had disappeared. The teacher looked thoroughly confused as he walked back to his desk. He stared up at the ceiling obviously trying to spot where the water leak had come from. All the class were in hysterics. They'd been so busy looking at the blackboard, they hadn't seen the cloud either. I could hear Gertie laughing; she really was pushing her luck.

The lesson continued. The teacher read page after page to the kids; it was really very boring. I nearly fell asleep myself three times. When he eventually put the book down, and turned to write something on the blackboard, I sensed that Gertie was casting another spell. A moment later, his book disappeared. Again the kids had been so busy looking at the blackboard, I doubt any of them noticed. When the teacher looked around, he stared at the empty desk.

"Who's taken my book?" he shouted. "Come on. Own up or I shall put you all in detention. Who did it?" As the teacher walked between the rows of desks, Gertie reversed the spell, and the book reappeared on the desk behind him.

All the other kids shouted, "It's behind you, sir."

The teacher turned around and looked in disbelief at the book.

"Someone here is messing around, and when I find out who it is, there'll be trouble."

I could feel Gertie's desk shaking with her laughter. She really was going far beyond what was acceptable. It was time to put my plan into action.

I waited until the lesson had ended. Just as I'd hoped, Gertie made her way to the loo. Once I was sure she was alone in there, I put in a call to Daze. I'd warned her that I'd be in touch, so she'd deliberately kept her diary free. The only thing I hadn't considered was whether my phone would work now it was shrunk. I crossed my fingers, and sure enough, it worked first time.

"Daze, it's me," I whispered.

"Are you ready for me?"

"Yeah. I assume you can track where I am?"

"Yeah, I've got you."

"Okay, come on over now."

"I'm on my way."

Gertie had washed her hands, and was walking over to

the drier when suddenly a thunderous noise filled the room. She looked around, terrified. There, in front of her, stood Daze.

"Are you Gertie Pride?" Daze said in her most serious voice.

"Ye-ye-yeah, who are you?"

"My name is Daze. I'm a Rogue Retriever."

All the colour drained from Gertie's face. "Oh?" Was all she could manage.

"I believe you've been abusing your magical powers in the human world."

"I only played a couple of jokes on—on the teacher," Gertie stammered.

"Magic is not a joking matter, young lady. You risk revealing yourself as a witch to the humans. That's strictly prohibited. Don't you know that?"

"Yes. I'm sorry."

"Sorry doesn't cut it."

"What are you going to do?"

"I should take you back to Candlefield, and throw you in jail. What would your parents think about that?"

For a moment, I thought that Gertie was going to cry, but she pulled herself together.

"They wouldn't be very pleased with me."

"Well then, what should I do with you?"

"Will you give me another chance, please?"

"How do I know you won't do the same thing again?"

"I won't. I promise. I won't do any more magic in Washbridge ever again."

"You *can* do magic in Washbridge. No one has said you can't. But you can't do it so openly, and you can't do it just for a laugh."

"I won't. Please don't take me back. Please don't put me in jail."

"Okay, but this is your one and only warning. Got it?"

"Got it."

"Okay." And with that Daze disappeared.

At the first opportunity, I sneaked out of Gertie's bag, made my way to the exit, and then reversed the 'shrink' spell.

Daze and I met up just outside the school grounds.

"How did I do?" she said. "Do you think she means it?"

"I think you convinced her. I don't think we'll have any more problems with Gertie Pride. I'm sure she'll think twice before she does any magic from now on. Thanks, Daze."

"Not a problem. I'd better get going. See you around."

***

I couldn't help myself. I just had to share my Luther news.

Ever A Wool Moment was absolutely buzzing, and when I caught up with Kathy, she looked extremely harassed.

"What do you want? I'm run off my feet."

"I have some really exciting news, and I wanted to share it with you."

"If you must."

"You could at least pretend to be interested."

"I am interested, what is it?"

"Luther has asked me out on a date."

"You cannot be serious! How can you keep deluding yourself like this?"

"This time it's different."

"It was different the last time, and the time before that."

"No, honestly. I bumped into him this morning, and the first thing he said was *'Call me Lou'*. He's never said that before; that must mean we've moved to the next level."

"The next level? You're not even on level one yet."

"Why would he say 'Call me Lou', if he didn't think we had some kind of relationship?"

"So that's it? You came all this way to tell me that Luther Stone said 'Call me Lou'?"

"No, of course not. Do you think I'm stupid? Don't answer that. He asked me to go out for dinner with him."

"You mean like last time? You, him and a cast of thousands?"

"There weren't *thousands*. There were ten at the most. Anyway, this time it's different. He said it was an *intimate* dinner for the two of us. See? Intimate—that's what he said."

"Okay. If you say so."

"It's the real thing this time."

"Does that mean you'll be buying yet another new dress?"

"I'm sure I can find something in my wardrobe."

"Look, I'd better get back to work. You won't forget you're taking Mikey to Coffee Triangle later, will you?"

"Don't worry. It's all in hand."

As I left the shop, I realised Kathy was right. I couldn't possibly go on my first 'official' date with Luther, sorry, I mean Lou, wearing something he'd seen before. I'd have to find the funds from somewhere to get a new outfit.

Chapter 8

Mrs V was alone behind the desk.

"Where's Mrs D?"

"My arm is much better now. I don't need D to act as my second arm anymore."

"That's good. Anything to report?"

"No, nothing. Except that I think there's something wrong with the heating."

"What's the problem?" It felt warm enough to me.

"It's okay out here, but when I went in to your office to feed the stupid cat, it was absolutely freezing in there. Has your radiator stopped working or something?"

"Not that I'm aware of."

"You'd better take a look at it. You don't want to catch a chill at your age."

My age? Cheek!

I went through to my office, but didn't notice any change of temperature at all. Winky was staring through the window, and totally ignored me as usual. I assumed he must be looking for Bella. Seeing him sitting there, reminded me that he hadn't used his little flags for a while. I kind of missed the feline semaphore.

"Jill." My mother suddenly appeared behind me.

"Hi, Mum. How are things in Ghost Town?"

"Fine, thanks. I've come to ask you a favour."

"Does it involve custard creams?"

"No, I've reached an agreement with Alberto. He understands that custard creams are my one vice, and so he's prepared to let me have them. He said if that was the only bad habit I had, then he could live with it. Which I think is very fair, don't you?"

"I do think it's fair, and if it means you don't eat *my* custard creams, then I'm all for it."

"I came to see you because there's someone I'd like you to meet."

"Who's that?"

I'd no sooner asked than another ghost appeared next to my mother. No wonder Mrs V had noticed a chill in my office.

"Jill, this is Priscilla."

"Nice to meet you, Priscilla."

"You too, Jill, your mother speaks very highly of you."

"How come I can see Priscilla?" I asked my mother.

"I thought it would help if she attached herself to you temporarily while we explained what it is she's after. It's much easier than me having to act as an intermediary."

"That makes sense. How exactly can I help you, Priscilla?"

"It's a little awkward." She looked embarrassed.

"Go on, Priscilla," my mother encouraged. "Spit it out. I'm sure Jill will be able to help."

"The thing is." Priscilla was avoiding eye contact. "There's someone — err"

"Oh dear, this could take all day," my mother said, impatiently. "There's a gentleman that Priscilla is quite attracted to."

"You mean a ghost?"

"Of course. Unfortunately, Priscilla's a little shy, and can't bring herself to speak to him."

"Okay, but I still don't see where I come in."

"You know the gentleman in question."

"I do?"

"Yes. It's someone who's only recently passed."

Then I realised who she was talking about. "You mean the colonel?"

Priscilla looked even more embarrassed.

"Yes, dear," my mother said. "Priscilla has got her eyes and her heart set on the colonel, but she's simply too shy to speak to him. I told her that you and the colonel had been good friends when he was alive."

"That's true."

"And so, we wondered if you might play Cupid?"

"I'd be happy to. I haven't seen him for a while, but the next time he pops in, I'll put in a word for you, Priscilla."

"Thank you, Jill." She was all smiles and giggles now.

"I can't promise anything, though."

"I understand, but if you'd just have a word with him, I'd be eternally grateful."

"Right then." My mother took Priscilla's hand. "We'd better get back to Ghost Town." And with that, the two of them disappeared.

So now I was moonlighting as a matchmaker for ghosts.

***

Kathy's problem was that she didn't know how to handle kids. Although I didn't have any of my own, I still felt I had the edge when it came to understanding them. Kathy's strategy was to shout at them. Shouting at Mikey, and telling him not to play his drum hadn't worked, but I had a carefully formulated plan which was guaranteed to get results. Mikey and I were on our way to Coffee Triangle. This was my genius, fool-proof plan to wean him off the drums. I was absolutely convinced that after he'd spent an hour or so in Coffee Triangle on drum day, he would never want to see another drum for the rest of his life.

Kathy had promised to make me a slap-up meal when we got back, by way of thanks.

Mikey was in the passenger seat—banging his stupid drum.

"Mikey!"

"Yes, Auntie Jill?"

"Do you think you could hold off on the drum for a while?"

"Don't you like it?"

"It's very good, but I've got a bit of a headache."

"The drum is very good for getting rid of headaches."

"What makes you think that?"

"Mum's always saying so."

"Are you sure she didn't say it *gave* her a headache?"

"I don't think so."

Bang, crash, thud, bang, crash, thud. It wasn't as if he had any sense of timing or rhythm; he just hit the thing randomly as hard as he could. By the time we arrived in town, my eardrums were ringing.

"Where is the coffee shop, Auntie Jill?"

"It's just around the corner, but you won't be able to take your drum in with you."

"Why not?"

"Those are the rules, I'm afraid. They have their own drums, and you have to use those."

"Okay, I guess."

"Give me yours and I'll put it in the boot."

"Are you sure it'll be safe in there?"

"Pretty sure. I don't think there are many toy drum

thieves wandering the streets of Washbridge."

"It's not a toy."

"Sorry. I'll put it in the boot anyway. It'll be perfectly safe in there."

We made our way down the street towards Coffee Triangle. When we were still fifty yards away, we could hear the banging and thudding. It was a wonder the council hadn't closed them down. It wasn't so bad on triangle or tambourine day, but on gong day, and particularly drum day, the noise was unbearable.

"I can hear them, Auntie Jill," Mikey said, getting more and more excited.

"It's horribly noisy isn't it, Mikey?"

"It sounds great!"

That wasn't the reaction I'd been hoping for. Still, once we were inside and he was actually exposed to that awful noise, he'd soon change his mind.

The place was as busy as ever; people seemed to like drum day. I guess a lot of people like to de-stress by banging a drum. Luckily, we managed to find a seat in a corner.

"Can I have a drum, Auntie Jill?"

"I'll ask at the counter. You stay there while I go and get some drinks, and see about getting you a drum."

Throughout the shop, the sound of the drumming was just unbelievable. My head was thumping. I glanced back at Mikey; surely it must be getting to him by now. But far from it. He was drumming on the table top—smiling and laughing—he seemed to be really enjoying himself. That wouldn't last for long. The noise would soon wear him down.

The poor man behind the counter looked traumatised.

"Can I have a medium, skinny latte, and a small Coke, please?"

He shook his head, and pointed to his ears. Then I realised he was wearing earplugs. Not a great idea for someone working behind a counter, but perhaps understandable given the circumstances. He took out a notepad and pen from his pocket, and put them on the counter in front of me. I scribbled my order; he nodded, and went to get our drinks.

I was about to ask him about the drum when I remembered he couldn't hear me, so I scribbled on the notepad again, 'Do you have any drums to spare?'

He went into the back room, and returned with one. Mikey was thrilled when he saw it.

I handed him the coke.

"Can I have the drum, Auntie Jill?"

"There you go."

He grabbed the drumsticks, and started beating the thing with all of his might. I was beginning to have serious doubts about my plan. I'd assumed that when the barrage of noise hit him, he'd beg me to take him home, but he seemed as happy as a lark.

Forty-five minutes later, he was still hammering away on the drum. My head was about to explode.

"Come on Mikey, it's time to go home now."

"Aww, Auntie Jill, I'm having fun."

"Sorry, but you're only allowed to stay for forty-five minutes. Other people want to have a go."

"I'm sure some of these people have been here longer than that," he said.

"Those are the rules. I'm sorry."

Before he could argue, I snatched the drum away from

him.

He sulked all the way back to the car. Just as we were about to set off he shouted, "Auntie Jill! Stop!"

"What is it Mikey?"

"Look there!" He pointed to a shop a few doors down from Coffee Triangle.

"You mean the music shop?"

"Yes. Can I look in there please, Auntie Jill?"

"I promised your mum we'd be back soon."

"Please. Just for five minutes. Please."

"Okay, but no longer."

He couldn't get out of the car quickly enough.

"Hi," the man behind the counter said. "Can I help?"

"My nephew would like to have a look around."

"Sure — help yourself."

Mikey made a beeline for the drums. He found a kit, sat down and started bashing away. My headache was getting worse by the minute. Over the next hour, he tried out every drum kit in the shop. I had to practically drag him out of there, kicking and screaming.

"Just ten more minutes, Auntie Jill. Just ten more minutes. Please!"

"No, I'm sorry. I have to get you home." I practically threw him into the car.

Kathy opened the door, and cringed when she saw that Mikey was still playing his drum.

"Did you have a good time Mikey?"

"It was great, Mum! Coffee Triangle is brilliant. Can I go there again?"

Kathy gave me a look.

"Maybe — one day," she said, through gritted teeth.

"And guess where else Auntie Jill took me?"

"I've no idea."

"To the music shop. They sell drum kits—lots of them. I played on them all. I've seen the drum kit I want for my birthday—or Christmas. Can I have it Mum? Can I?"

"We'll see, Mikey. Go through and tell your dad all about it."

"Maybe I'll skip dinner, Kathy." I started for the door.

"Whoa there, Missy. You're not going anywhere." Kathy grabbed me by the shoulder. "I thought your cunning plan was meant to wean him off the drum? Now, not only is he *still* playing the drum, but he wants me to take him to Coffee Triangle to play one there, *and* he's picked out the drum kit he wants for his birthday or Christmas."

"Yeah, things didn't *quite* go according to plan."

"You think?"

Chapter 9

"Remind me again why I'm making you dinner?" Kathy said. "Oh, yes. I remember now. It's for getting Mikey to stop playing the drum."

"I did my best."

"And on a scale of nought to epic fail, you hit the jackpot."

"Give her a break." Peter grinned.

"Thanks, Peter." It was time to change the subject. "How's the new business going?"

"I'm getting there; it's nice to be my own boss. I do miss the colonel though."

"Me too." Little did he know that I was about to play matchmaker to the colonel. "What's for dinner, Kathy?" I was starving.

"Chicken," she shouted from the kitchen. "Not that you deserve it."

I did love a nice piece of chicken.

"It's Wilma, actually." Kathy came through carrying a huge plate.

"Wilma?"

"You know: the chicken that got out when the kids went next door. The one that you chased around."

"No! Please tell me you haven't killed one of the chickens from next door."

"Of course not." She grinned. "The neighbours killed it for us."

"Take it away. I don't want it. Give me baked beans on toast. I can't eat Wilma."

Kathy burst into laughter. "I'm only joking. It's from the supermarket."

"I'm not sure I believe you."

"Follow me." She led me through to the kitchen and showed me the packaging.

"Do you believe me now?"

"I guess so."

"So, let me get this right. You don't mind eating *this* chicken, because you didn't know it personally. But if it had been Wilma—"

"Just serve me the chicken."

"I was just telling Jill," Peter said. "I'm enjoying working for myself, but I miss the colonel."

"He was a lovely old man." Kathy had joined us at the table. "It was a terrible way to go, such a tragedy. I'm surprised you aren't more upset about it, Jill. You were quite close to him."

"I miss him too."

It was hard to be upset about losing someone when you were still in regular contact with them, but of course I couldn't tell Kathy that.

The meal, as always, was delicious. Wilma or not, the chicken was very tasty, and the dessert, strawberry cheesecake, was absolutely to die for.

"Thanks, Kathy. That was delicious."

"When are *you* going to invite me and Pete over to *your* place for dinner?"

"Err—I don't know. Soon."

"Well, let me think. How many times have you invited us for dinner to-date? Oh yeah—that would be none."

"You know me, I'm not very good in the kitchen. Whereas you're brilliant."

"Flattery will get you nowhere."

"It's done okay so far."

"Anyway, there's something I wanted to tell you," Kathy said.

"What now?"

"Don't panic; it's nothing bad. It's called fun."

"Your idea of fun and mine are very different. What have you signed me up for this time?"

"There's a fancy dress party—"

"I hate fancy dress."

"You hate everything. You, me, and Pete are going to the party."

"But Kathy—"

"You're going, and that's all there is to it. As your older sister, it's my responsibility to see that you have fun whether you want to or not. Anyway, it sounds really good. The theme is 'things that go bump in the night'."

"What does that even mean?"

"You know: ghosts and vampires and witches. Spooky things like that."

Oh no.

"Anyway, we've decided: Peter's going to go as a werewolf, I'm going to go as a vampire, and we thought you could go as a witch."

"I'd make a terrible witch."

"I think you'd be a great witch. You have the nose for it."

"What do you mean I have the nose for it? There's nothing wrong with my nose. I have a cute nose."

"Hmm? Looks a bit witch-like to me." Kathy laughed.

***

I'd phoned Tony Bow a thousand times, but he

obviously had no intention of answering or returning my calls. If I wanted to speak to him, I'd just have to confront him at his house. So, bright and early the next morning, I went straight over there, but when I knocked on the door, it was a woman who answered.

"Is Tony in?"

"If you're another one of his *fancy* women, you're out of luck."

"No, nothing like that. My name is Jill Gooder. I'm a private investigator."

"Well, whoever you are — he isn't here."

"Do you know when he'll be back?"

"I don't know, and I don't care. Never, probably."

"I'm investigating the murder of Carly Baxter."

"Terrible business. But what does it have to do with Tony?"

"Maybe nothing, but I need to speak to him."

"Well, like I said. He doesn't live here. I've thrown him out. Good riddance."

"Can I ask why?"

"I don't see why not. Everyone will know sooner or later. He's been having yet another affair. I found this." She put her hand in her pocket, and pulled out a gold necklace with a single red stone. "It was in his car. Of course, the lying rat denied any knowledge of it. He said he didn't know how it got there. Yeah, right! I've had enough of his cheating. This isn't the first time. I told him to get out and never come back."

"Do you know where he might have gone?"

"I don't know, and I don't care."

"Please! Is there anywhere you can think of where I might find him?"

"He's probably gone to his brother's. That's where he usually goes when we have an argument. Only this time, he won't be coming back."

It took me a while, but eventually, I managed to persuade her to let me have Tony Bow's brother's address.

Before I went in search of Tony Bow, I decided to speak with Gerry Baxter. Unsurprisingly, he was a mess. He looked as though he hadn't shaved in days, and he smelled of the previous night's booze.

"Mr Baxter. Could I have a few words?"

"Who are you? Press? I've nothing to say to you."

"I'm not the press."

"Police? Why didn't you do something while she was still alive instead of wasting time questioning me? She might still be here if you had."

I saw no reason to correct him. If he thought I was the police, that might work in my favour.

"I know this is difficult for you, Mr Baxter, but we're just trying to find the person who murdered your wife."

"If I get my hands on the scumbag, I'll kill him."

"Do you have any idea what might have happened to her after she disappeared?"

"No. It doesn't make any sense. She was meant to lie low just long enough for me to get the story into the papers, and then we were going to meet up again."

"Where were you supposed to meet?"

"I've already told your people all of this."

"If you wouldn't mind going over it one more time, I'd be grateful."

"We'd arranged to meet in Black Woods, but she didn't show up."

"Is there anyone you can think of who might have wanted to harm Carly?"

He laughed, but it was a hollow laugh. "No one. Everyone loved her. This is all my fault. I came up with the stupid publicity stunt idea. If I hadn't, then none of this would have happened."

"What about Tony Bow?"

"What about him?" he snapped.

"Didn't you suspect that he and Carly were having an affair?"

"Carly and Tony Bow? Are you serious? Of course she wasn't having an affair with him. She couldn't stand the man. Neither of us could. We were in love. There's no way Carly would have had an affair with anyone. And certainly not with Tony Bow. Not if he was the last man on earth."

I took the necklace out of my pocket. "Do you recognise this?"

"It's Carly's." He snatched it from me, and held it to his heart. "It was her lucky charm." He broke down in tears. "Wasn't so lucky, was it?"

"When was the last time you saw her wearing it?"

"She wore it every day."

"Was she wearing it on the day that she jumped from the bridge?"

"Yes. Like I said, it was her lucky charm."

Before I left, I managed to persuade him to let me hold onto the necklace; I promised to return it as soon as I could.

***

If Carly Baxter had been wearing the necklace when she jumped off the bridge, then the only way it could have been in Tony Bow's car was if he'd seen her after she'd left the site of the bungee jump.

On my way over to Tony Bow's brother's house, I gave Jack Maxwell a call.

"Jack. I'm fairly sure that Tony Bow murdered Carly Baxter."

"You mean the guy who owns 'Jump To It'?"

"Yeah, that's the guy."

"Why do you think that?"

"His wife found a necklace in the back seat of his car. I've just spoken to Gerry Baxter who's confirmed that it was Carly's. She wore it every day; she called it her lucky charm. And what's more, he's absolutely certain that she was wearing it on the day she jumped off the bridge."

"How does Tony Bow come to have it, then?"

"I don't know. But I intend to find out. I'm on my way over to his brother's place now."

"Give me the address, and I'll be there as soon as I can. Don't do anything stupid in the meantime, Jill."

"Do I ever?"

It was Tony Bow who answered the door at his brother's house.

"What do *you* want? I've got nothing else to say to you. I've got enough problems without you coming around here."

I held up the necklace. "Do you recognise this?"

"I should do. It got me thrown out of my own home."

"So you don't deny that you had it?"

"Belle said she found it in the back seat of my car, but I

don't know how it got there."

"You know it belonged to Carly Baxter, I assume?"

The expression on his face told me that he didn't.

"Carly? Are you sure?" He was clearly taken aback.

"Absolutely. I've just been speaking to Gerry. He said that she was wearing it on the day she jumped off the bridge."

"I don't understand. I'd never seen it until Belle found it in the car. I didn't put it there, and Carly has never been in my car."

"So are you denying that you've seen Carly since the day she disappeared?"

"I haven't seen her for ages. And I certainly haven't seen her since she went missing. What are you accusing me of?"

I didn't get a chance to answer because Jack Maxwell and three other police officers turned up, and took Tony Bow into custody.

Job done. So, why did I still have a nagging doubt about this case?

Chapter 10

My phone rang.

"Jill, it's Amber. We're over at Mum's. Can you come over now? It's important."

"What's happened? Amber?"

She'd already hung up.

You could never be sure with the twins. Their idea of an emergency and mine were miles apart. But what if something serious had happened? I daren't risk it, so I magicked myself over to Aunt Lucy's. When I arrived, Aunt Lucy and the twins were sitting at the kitchen table enjoying a cup of tea and *my* custard creams.

"I'm sorry, Jill. I just ran out," Aunt Lucy said. "I'd go and fetch you some from the shop, but my knees are playing up. I do have a few digestives, though."

"It's okay. Anyway, I thought there was some sort of emergency over here. It doesn't look much like an emergency to me."

"It most certainly is," Amber said. "Sit down."

Pearl took a deep breath. "I'm sorry to have to tell you this, Jill, but Jethro has been signed up by a male modelling agency."

"Sorry? What?"

"I said—Jethro has been signed up by a male modelling agency."

"And that's your idea of an emergency?"

"He won't be doing Mum's garden anymore," Amber said, obviously exasperated by my indifference. "There'll be no more Jethro time."

"And that's why you dragged me over here?"

"Don't pretend you didn't enjoy Jethro time," Pearl

said. "You know you did."

"He is a good looking man, and I can understand why a model agency would sign him up, but I would hardly class this as an emergency."

"So what would you call it?" Pearl demanded.

"A tad disappointing, maybe. Certainly nothing to trouble the emergency services with. So who's going to do your garden, Aunt Lucy?"

"Jethro said he wouldn't leave me in the lurch, and that he'd already passed my name on to someone called Sebastian."

"Who cares about Sebastian?" Amber pouted. "We want Jethro time."

Just then, there was a knock on the door. Pearl was closest, so she went to see who it was. Amber still looked depressed; even Aunt Lucy looked a bit downhearted. When Pearl came back, she was wide-eyed, and appeared to have been rendered speechless.

"What is it, Pearl?" Aunt Lucy said.

Pearl opened her mouth to speak, but no words came out.

"Pearl? What's going on?" Amber said.

"It's — err — it's Sebastian. He's at the front door."

"Well, don't just leave him standing there," Aunt Lucy said. "Show him in."

"Err — yeah. Okay." Moments later, she returned with the most handsome hunk I had ever seen.

"I just wanted to check if it's okay to start on the garden today," he said, in the sexiest voice I had ever heard. "Jethro said that he'd cleared it with you, but I didn't want to make a start until I'd checked, personally. Is that okay?" He looked at the four drooling women in front of him. "So—is it okay for me to start?"

Aunt Lucy was the first to shake herself out of the stupor. "Yes, absolutely. You can start straight away. Would you like a drink? A piece of cake? Or some custard creams? I could go and fetch you some from the shop."

Charming! Whatever happened to her iffy knees?

***

I'd promised to meet Kathy and Peter outside Coffee Triangle. We were going to pick out our fancy dress costumes.

"Where's Peter?"

"He got a job at the last minute. He can't make it."

"Does that mean he's not going to the fancy dress party? If *he's* not going, *I'm* not going."

"Pete *is* going. He'll have to get his costume later today or tomorrow."

"Where is this place anyway?" I moaned. "This had better not take long. It's my date with Lou tonight."

"Don't panic. You won't be late for *Looooooo*." Kathy mocked. "The shop is just around the corner."

Party Poppers sold absolutely everything to do with parties. There were balloons, streamers, party poppers (obviously), and costumes of every type imaginable. As soon as I stepped inside, I sensed that the people working in there weren't human. They were sups; all three of them. One was a vampire, one a wizard, and the other, a werewolf. They'd clearly sensed I was a sup too; I could tell from the knowing looks they gave me.

"How can I help you, madam?" the young female vampire asked Kathy.

"We're going to a fancy dress party. I'm looking for a vampire outfit, and my sister is looking for a witch's outfit."

The young vampire laughed, but then checked herself.

"Is something the matter?" Kathy said.

"Err—no. Sorry, madam. The vampire outfits are just here, and the witch's outfits are over there. Perhaps you'd like to take a look at these while I help your sister?"

"Okay," Kathy agreed. "You go with her, Jill, and make sure you pick something nice."

I followed the vampire to the far corner of the shop. "What are you doing?" she said when she'd made sure we were alone.

"Buying a fancy dress outfit."

"But you *are* a witch."

"I *know* I'm a witch, but my sister doesn't. She's a human."

"How can you be sisters if she's human?"

"I was adopted."

"Was it her idea for you to go to the fancy dress party as a witch?"

"What do *you* think?"

"That's too funny."

"I'm glad you think so. It's unusual to find a shop in Washbridge staffed entirely by sups. Do you three own this place?"

"I wish. The owners are a witch and a wizard who live in Candlefield. Charlie manages this place; Neil and me just work here. The three of us share a flat too; a loft here in Washbridge."

"Doesn't it get a bit much working and living together?"

"It can do." She pointed to the rack of costumes next to her. "These are all the witch outfits we have."

"Is this some kind of joke?"

"What's wrong?"

"Look at these. No self-respecting witch would wear these. They're way too skimpy. Where are the authentic witch outfits?"

The vampire looked around again to make sure we still couldn't be overheard.

"When we first opened the shop, we stocked nothing but authentic witch costumes, but nobody would hire them. Everyone said, *'That's not what witches wear'*. What could we do? We knew it was exactly what witches wore, but if we'd stuck to our guns, we'd have been bankrupt within the first few months. So, in the end, we had to look at what all the other shops were doing, and copy them. These are really popular."

"But they're nothing like what a witch would wear."

"I know, but it's all we've got. I'll leave you to choose one. I'd better go and see how your sister's doing."

I worked my way through the shelf of *so-called* witch costumes, and picked out the least skimpy one I could find. It was still a good three inches shorter than I would have liked, and way too low on the neckline, but it was the best I could do. I grabbed a hat too. That was just as ridiculous; all bendy and crumpled. No Candlefield witch would have been seen dead in it.

When I caught up with Kathy and the vampire, Kathy was trying out some false fangs.

"Duy thes lick lack rail fungs?" she mumbled, through a mouth full of fangs.

"Sorry, madam." The vampire looked puzzled. "I can't

tell what you're saying."

Kathy slipped the fangs out of her mouth. "I said, do these look like real fangs? Jill? What do you think?"

I shrugged.

The vampire opened her mouth and I could see her real fangs. She turned to Kathy and said, "Look, they look realistic on me, don't they?"

Kathy stared into the vampire's mouth and nodded. "They do look much better than I thought they would. Go on then, I'll take these."

We paid for our outfits, and on our way out, Kathy said, "My husband will be in later. He's going to the party as a werewolf. Do you have plenty of werewolf costumes?"

"Dozens. Tell him to ask for Charlie. He's our werewolf expert." She pointed to the man standing close to the door.

Charlie was way more than just an expert.

***

The little black number hadn't been very lucky for me. This time I'd gone for a little red number, and although I say it myself, I looked super sexy in it. Lou had called me during the day to confirm he'd reserved a table at Hotel Lake, which was one of the top hotels in Washbridge; it was a four-star, if I wasn't mistaken. Its restaurant had an excellent reputation.

We'd arranged to meet in the bar. I arrived a few minutes early; Luther turned up shortly after.

"Jill, you look stunning. Have you been here before?"

"No, this is my first time, but I've heard the food is really good."

"Shall we have a drink before we go through?"

"That would be lovely. I'll have a small glass of dry, white wine, please."

Luther called the barman over and ordered the drinks. Then he took a handkerchief from his pocket, and began to rub the metal bar rail. How strange? Still, I guess everyone has their unusual habits. After a few minutes, we made our way through to the restaurant. The maître d' showed us to a quiet table in a corner. As we studied the menu, I could see Luther seemed rather distracted.

"Is anything the matter, Lou?"

"No, nothing. Have you decided what you'd like to eat yet?"

"I'm happy to go with whatever you recommend."

Luther ordered for both of us. We chatted while we waited for our meals to be served, but again I could sense he was a little distracted. After a few moments, he took out his handkerchief, and began to rub the leg of the table.

"I must say I'm a little disappointed," he said. "A four-star hotel like this. You'd think they'd know how to keep these surfaces looking good. Really, it's inexcusable. Don't you think?"

"I guess so, yeah." Huh?

He continued to polish the table legs. I couldn't begin to understand why he was so interested in the finish of the metalwork.

Our food arrived, and it was indeed excellent. We had salmon, which melted in the mouth. Eat your heart out, Winky! That was followed by Eton mess. I couldn't have managed another morsel.

"That was absolutely gorgeous," I said, as we sipped our coffee. "Thank you so much, Lou."

"My pleasure, Jill. You've been delightful company. I'm just sorry that the state of the metalwork has rather tarnished the evening."

"I can't say that I'd noticed it."

There was something very puzzling about all this. Why was Luther so obsessed with the finish of the metalwork? It was only chrome after all.

Chrome! That was it! I remembered now.

When I'd been at Luther's flat, I'd noticed that most of his furniture was chrome and glass. In fact, I'd never seen so much chrome. When I mentioned it, he'd said that his brother worked at—where was it now? Oh yeah, of course—Chrome City, that was it. Luther said his brother had given him a good deal.

Oh no! It couldn't be. Could it?

"Lou?"

"Yes, Jill?"

"Can I ask what your brother does for a living?"

"Luther? He's an accountant, didn't you know?"

"And you?"

"I work at Chrome City."

"So you're twins?"

"That's right. I thought you knew."

"And what's your full first name?"

"It's Louis. You look confused, Jill."

"No, not at all."

Oh bum!

***

Lou dropped me back at my flat. I got the distinct impression he was hoping to come in for a night cap, but I said I had a headache and needed an early night.

Lou wasn't Luther. Lou was Louis. Although they were identical in appearance, Louis didn't have Luther's sex appeal. And, who wants to listen to someone talk about chrome all night long? Not me. Compared to Lou, Luther the accountant seemed positively exciting.

I'd no sooner got back inside my flat than the phone rang. It was Kathy. I was tempted to ignore it, but I knew that she'd catch up with me sooner or later. I might as well face the music now.

"Hi." Was all I could manage.

"Oh dear. You sound happy — not! I assume tonight wasn't a success. He didn't stand you up, did he?"

"Of course not."

"So what happened?"

I considered lying, but it would have been pointless. Kathy could always tell.

"It wasn't Luther."

"What wasn't Luther?"

"The man I went on the date with, wasn't Luther."

"You're not making any sense, Jill. I thought you said he asked you out on a date — just the two of you?"

"Lou did. Luther didn't."

"I'm confused."

"It turns out that Luther has a twin brother called Louis who likes to be called Lou."

"Oh no. That's too funny." Kathy laughed. "You could not make this stuff up. Pete, come and listen to this. Jill's just been on a date with someone she thought was her heart throb, Luther, but who turned out to be his twin brother, Louis. Have I got that right, Jill?"

"Yes, but I don't know why you two are laughing."

"Come on, Jill, even you must see the funny side."

"Not really, no. I've just spent the last few hours listening to someone talk about chrome."

"Chrome?"

"Don't ask. I'm going to bed. Goodnight."

Chapter 11

Even though Tony Bow had been arrested, and was likely to be charged with murder, something about the Carly Baxter case was still bugging me. On a hunch, I'd arranged to meet Jean Cumberland again in Coffee Triangle. It was maracas day.

"Hi again." She shook her maracas. "I'm happy to help, but I'm sure I've already told you everything I remember about that day."

"I just have one very quick question." I held out the necklace. "Do you recognise this?"

"No, should I?"

"It belonged to the woman who went missing."

"I heard on the news that a woman's body has been found. Was it her?"

"I'm afraid so. Please take another look at the necklace. Are you sure you don't remember seeing her wearing it that day?"

"I don't, sorry. But then I doubt if I would have noticed."

"Okay, thanks anyway." I made to leave.

"Wait a minute," she called after me. "We did take a few photos that day. Everyone took turns to take a group picture. The woman will probably be in them. Let me just check."

Jean flicked through the photographs on her smartphone. "Yes, there, look—she *is* wearing it."

In the photograph Carly Baxter could be seen standing with the customers. And there, around her neck was the necklace with the red stone in it. Gerry Baxter had been right; she had been wearing it on that day.

**

When I got back to the office, Mrs V began to scramble around, and shoved something into the top drawer of her desk. She looked red in the face and very flustered.

"Are you all right, Mrs V?"

"Err—yes, I'm fine. Absolutely fine, Jill. Nothing wrong with me."

She didn't look absolutely fine. In fact, she looked very guilty. She'd clearly been up to something she didn't want me to know about. I was intrigued. Had she been reading "Hot Knitters Monthly" or "Raunchy Yarns"? Mrs V was obviously more of a dark horse than I'd realised.

"Are you sure there's nothing you want to tell me, Mrs V?"

"Only that there's been a strange noise coming from your office."

"Did you take a look to see what it was?"

"I'm not going in there. That cat of yours might have turned into a werecat again."

"Hmm, yeah, I don't think that actually happened."

"What about when his fur grew really long?"

"That was just the ointment."

I stood and listened for a few moments. "You're right, I *can* hear something. It sounds like some kind of motor. I'll go and see what it is."

I braced myself as I slowly opened the door, and peered in.

"What the—?"

I stepped inside, and closed the door behind me. There was no need for Mrs V to witness this.

Over by the window was a mini treadmill. And, guess who was on it? That's right. You got it in one! My darling, psycho cat, Winky, who was wearing a fetching red and yellow headband, and listening to music on his headphones.

He could barely get his breath, and looked as though he was about to collapse.

"Winky! What are you doing?"

He was lost in music.

"Winky!" I tried again, but it was no good—he couldn't hear a thing.

I lifted one of the headphones, and then released it so it sprang back onto his ear—that got his attention. Shaking his head, and still a little dazed, he jumped off the treadmill.

"What do you think you're playing at?" he yelled.

"I tried to get your attention, but you couldn't hear me."

"You didn't have to burst my eardrums!"

"Sorry about that."

"I've a good mind to sue you for the damage to my ear. If you had any money, I would."

"What's the treadmill for?"

"You run on it. The concept isn't that difficult to understand."

"I know what a treadmill is. I want to know why you have one."

"You're to blame."

"Me? Why?"

"You're the one who said I was fat."

It was true. I *had* said that when he'd suggested he might bungee jump, but I hadn't realised he'd taken it so much to heart.

"So you've bought a treadmill?"

"Actually, *you've* bought a treadmill."

"You used my credit card again?"

"Of course."

"I've only just paid off the last bill!"

"What else was I supposed to do? If you'd get me my own credit card, I wouldn't need to borrow yours."

"Who would pay your credit card bill?"

"You, of course."

"Right. And how much did this thing cost?"

"Don't panic. I haven't bought it. It's on hire, from hireafelinetreadmill.com."

"There isn't such a thing."

"Want to bet?"

***

Grandma had left a message that she wanted to see me, so I made my way over to Ever A Wool Moment. Kathy was run off her feet, as usual, so we just exchanged a quick '*hi*'. Grandma was in the back office, drumming her fingers on the desk.

"You took your time, didn't you?"

"I only just got your message."

"Take a seat. There's something I need to discuss with you."

What had I done this time? No doubt I was in trouble for something or other.

"We're coming up to the Levels AGM," Grandma said, as though I knew what she was talking about.

"The what?"

"AGM. You do know what AGM stands for, don't

you?"

"Annual General Meeting?"

"Very good! The Levels AGM is attended by all of the level six witches."

"I see."

"I have a lot of preparation to do for the meeting, so your sister is going to have to look after Ever for the next day or so."

Poor old Kathy. Snigger.

"And you will be accompanying me to the AGM."

What? "Me? Why me?"

"Because I say so."

"But didn't you just say that it was for level six witches?"

"I did."

"Doesn't that mean that only level six witches can attend?"

"Broadly speaking, yes. But every level six witch is allowed to take one assistant with them; you will be my assistant."

"How long is all of this going to take? I'm very busy."

"The AGM is only one day. You'll just have to reshuffle your other work. The main item on the agenda this year is the possible introduction of a new level. Level Seven."

Suddenly, I recalled the words I'd heard the pendant say to me '*You will take it to a new level*'.

"Hello?" Grandma shouted. "Have you dozed off?"

"Sorry, Grandma. I was miles away. Where do you stand on the proposal to introduce a new level?"

"I support the motion. In my opinion, there are way too many witches already at the top level, and some of them are totally inept. By introducing a new level, we can ensure only a truly elite witch will attain the highest level. So, you see, I have a lot of work to do, and I'll need you to help me to prepare my case. And, on the day, you'll be my girl Friday. You'll do whatever I need you to, so that I can focus on the debate itself. Okay?"

"Sure." Like I had a choice.

***

It was the evening of the fancy dress party. I knew there was no point in trying to get out of it because no matter what excuse I dreamed up, Kathy would see straight through it—just like she'd seen through my fake broken toe.

I'd agreed to meet her and Peter outside the local community hall where the party was being held. Even though I'd resigned myself to having to be there, there was no way I was going to wear that skimpy, so-called witch outfit that I'd borrowed from the shop. It was horrible. No self-respecting witch would have been seen dead in it. Instead, I was wearing an authentic outfit; similar to the one I'd worn for the Levels competition. And, although I say it myself, I looked every inch the witch.

"What's that you're wearing?" Kathy pulled a face.

"It's an authentic witch costume."

"Don't be ridiculous. You don't look anything like a witch. Where's the one you got from the shop?"

"I'm not wearing that thing. It was cheap and tacky."

"That's the idea. Anyway, it wasn't cheap and tacky; it was sexy."

"Witches aren't supposed to be sexy. Being a witch is a

very serious business."

Kathy looked at me nonplussed. "You do know that witches aren't real, don't you?"

"Yeah, of course I do."

"I suppose we'll just have to make the best of it." Kathy sighed. "What do you think of my outfit?"

"Tell me again what you're meant to be."

"Cheek! I'm a vampire, obviously."

She opened her mouth to show me her fangs, which looked plastic and quite ridiculous.

"Very scary. Don't bite my neck, will you?"

"What do you think to Pete's outfit?"

Peter looked very uncomfortable in the werewolf costume, and about as excited about the party as I did.

"You look very scary, Mr Werewolf."

He rolled his eyes.

"Come on then," Kathy said. "Let's go in. And try to remember, Jill, you're here to have *fun*. F-U-N."

Inside, it was packed with people dressed as every kind of supernatural creature you could imagine. There were dozens of witches, vampires and werewolves. But there were also ghosts and goblins, and some that I simply didn't recognise at all. Of course, none of them looked like real sups. But then, how could humans know what a sup really looked like?

Mercifully, there was a bar, so I sneaked over there on the pretence of going to the toilet. While I was at the bar enjoying a small vodka, I noticed a familiar face: a young woman dressed as a vampire. Where did I know her from? When she got a little closer, I sensed she really *was* a vampire. Then it clicked; it was the young woman who had served us in the fancy dress shop. She had a strange expression on her face. What was it? Then I realised—it was a look of hunger. And, if I wasn't mistaken, she was looking for a meal of human blood.

This was not good. I had to do something, so I grabbed my phone, and made a quick call to Daze.

"Jill? Where are you? It's very noisy there. I can hardly hear you."

"I'm in Washbridge at the community hall. At a fancy dress party."

"Oh right."

"The theme is 'things that go bump in the night'."

"What's your costume?"

"I was dreading you asking me that. I came as a witch."

"Oh dear, how ironic," she said.

"I rang because I think we may have a problem. I've just spotted a real vampire, and I'm absolutely sure she's on the hunt for human blood. I wondered if you could pop over because I have a horrible feeling something bad is about to happen."

"Okay. I was just about to wash my hair, but that can wait. I'll be with you shortly."

True to her word, a few minutes later, Daze tapped me on the shoulder.

"That was quick."

"Yeah, well it's not like I was busy. Where's this vampire?" She looked around the room.

"I don't know. She disappeared while I was calling you. I'm worried she might have already found a victim. Come on. We have to find her."

We pushed our way through the crowd, and it was Daze who eventually spotted her.

"There! Is that her?"

I nodded.

The vampire was walking hand in hand with a young man. They were headed towards the back exit. The look on the young man's face told me that he thought he'd got lucky. How wrong could he be?

Daze and I set off in pursuit. The door opened onto a dark alleyway, but there was just enough light to see that the young man was pinned against the wall with a look of terror on his face. The vampire had her mouth open, and her fangs extended. She was just about to sink them into his neck when Daze took out her net, and threw it over her. The vampire disappeared in a puff of smoke; the young man looked stunned.

"I'll see to him," I said, as I cast the 'forget' spell. The man shook his head as he no doubt tried to figure out why he was outside.

"I'd go back inside if I were you, young man," Daze said. "It's rather cold out here."

"Err, yeah, I guess I will." He scuttled off.

"Thanks for that, Daze."

"No problem. I'll pop over to Candlefield to book this one in, and then get back to washing my hair. See you around, Jill."

When I went back inside, Kathy was waiting for me by the door. "What were you doing outside with that young man, Jill?"

"I wasn't with him. I was just getting some fresh air."

"Says you. Looks like you were after a toy boy to me."

Chapter 12

Tony Bow was in custody, and likely to stand trial for the murder of Carly Baxter. So, why couldn't I shake the idea that I'd missed something? There was one aspect of the case in particular which simply didn't make sense: Why would he take Carly Baxter's necklace after he'd killed her? He must have realised that if it was found in his possession, it would incriminate him.

I went back to see Tony Bow's wife.

"Oh, it's you." She was obviously delighted to see me. "You got Tony arrested."

"That was down to the necklace."

"I would never have given it to you if I'd known you were going to use it to frame him for murder."

"You don't think he did it?"

"Tony? Kill someone? He doesn't have it in him. He might be a cheating scumbag, but he isn't a murderer. Why are you here anyway?"

"I'm not convinced your husband killed Carly. Would you mind showing me where you found the necklace?"

"What good will that do? The police have already been over the car with a fine toothcomb."

"Even so. If you wouldn't mind?"

She sighed, but went to collect the car keys.

"How come he didn't take the car when he went to his brother's house?"

"Tony hardly ever drives it. He mostly uses the van." She unlocked the doors. "He spends more time polishing it than he does driving it. He thinks more about that car than he does about me."

I opened the back door, and scrambled inside.

"I'll leave you to it," she said. "Let me have the keys back when you're finished."

What did I hope to find that the police hadn't already uncovered? I wasn't sure, but I had to give it a go. When Belle had gone back into the house, I shrunk myself so I could search even the smallest nook and cranny.

After an hour, I'd found precisely nothing, so I reversed the 'shrink' spell, and was about to lock the car when I spotted the air freshener hanging from the rear view mirror.

Then everything made sense.

***

Alison Shine looked surprised to see me.

"Hello, Alison. Could you spare me a few minutes, please?"

"Of course. I wanted to thank you for helping to find Carly's murderer. I feel bad now for pointing the finger at Gerry."

"Do you? Really?"

"Of course I do. He may not have been a good husband to Carly, but I shouldn't have accused him of her murder. How long will Bow get? They ought to throw away the key."

"That's up to the courts. If it gets that far."

"What do you mean? Why wouldn't it?"

"You tell me."

"You're talking in riddles."

"Are you still working at the car wash?"

"Yes." She looked puzzled. "Why do you ask?"

"It's ages since I used a car wash. They never seem to get my car as clean as I can. And what's with those air fresheners they insist on giving you? They smell awful, don't they? Do you hand those out?"

"Yes. Look, what's this all about?"

"Does Tony Bow have his car valeted at your place?"

Her face flushed red. "Maybe. I don't know. What's that got to do with anything?"

"I bet if I checked the records, I'd find he had it valeted once a week—regular as clockwork. He's that kind of man. You know the type—they prefer to polish their car rather than actually drive it. Don't you hate people like that?"

"Look. I have to get on. I'm meant to be meeting someone shortly."

"That's why you had to wait, isn't it?"

"Wait for what?"

"Wait until Tony Bow brought his car in for a valet. You had to keep Carly alive until then, didn't you?"

"I don't know what you're talking about."

"I'll bet the records show that Tony Bow brought his car in for a valet on the same day as Carly was murdered. Would you care for a small wager?"

Her legs seemed to buckle, and she had to put her hand on the wall to steady herself.

"That's when you planted the necklace, isn't it?"

She began to sob.

"Why did you kill her, Alison?"

"You wouldn't understand."

"Try me."

"She ruined my life. Not that I've ever had a life. She

saw to that. I was the one who had to stay at home to look after Dad while she went off and did her own thing — found herself a man, got married, started her own business. Everything was just dandy for Carly. She never once offered to help me; she just didn't care. But I was prepared to put up with it because I thought Dad would show his appreciation when the time came. But, then he told me was going to make a Will, and split everything fifty/fifty between us. Why should she have half? She's never looked after Dad. She's never done anything to help. And it's not like she needs the money. I do. I've got nothing. It isn't fair."

"So you decided to kill her?"

"No. It wasn't like that. But when she told me about that stupid stunt of hers I was so angry. She said they would make a fortune from the publicity. Like she didn't have enough money already. I saw red."

"How did you get her to come to your place?"

"Gerry had said she should hide out in Black Woods, but she didn't want to have to deal with the cold — she was always nesh. I said she could stay at my place until the newspapers had run the article, and then she could contact Gerry."

"How did you persuade her to stay? Surely Gerry must have tried to get in touch with her?"

"Carly always did like a drink. I just added a few pills to the mix."

"Then you came to see me."

"Yes, after I'd called the police. I had you fooled, didn't I?" Her tears had been replaced by a manic grin. "I had them all fooled."

"I think we should go inside now, Alison." I took her

arm, and led her into the living room, and then took out my phone.

"Who are you calling?"

"The police."

"But who will look after Dad?"

***

I was feeling ultra-guilty about Barry. It was ages since I'd taken him for a walk. He was at Aunt Lucy's, so I decided to pop over, have a quick cup of tea with her, and then take him for a walk in the park.

"Do you know much about the Levels AGM, Aunt Lucy?"

"I've been there a few times, but only as an assistant to your grandmother."

"*You* usually go with her?"

"Yes. I'm expecting her to ask me any day now. She always leaves it until the last minute."

"Oh?"

"What's wrong, dear?"

"She's asked me to be her assistant."

"Really?"

"I don't want to do it. I'm quite happy for you to be her assistant. I'll tell Grandma I'd rather not go with her."

"Don't do that. I have absolutely no desire to go to that stupid event. I'm just a little surprised, that's all. I've never seen any witch there who was below level five."

"That doesn't sound good. Is it even allowed?"

"I'm pretty sure there's no rule that specifies who can and can't attend, but it does seem common practice that the assistants are level five witches."

"Will you have a word with Grandma for me, and say that you'll go instead."

"Sorry, Jill, but if she's decided she wants to take you, nothing I or anyone else, says is going to change her mind. I'm afraid you're stuck with this one."

"Great."

As soon as we reached the park, and before Barry could run off like he usually did, another Labradoodle came charging towards us.

"Hi," the dog said. "I'm Barbara, but everybody calls me Babs."

"I'm Barry. Everyone calls me Barry. I like to walk."

"Me too. I love to walk."

"I like to come to the park."

"Me too."

"I like to eat."

"Me too!" Babs said. "We have so much in common."

As Barry and Babs continued their fascinating conversation, I noticed a young female vampire walking towards us. Judging by her obvious exhaustion, I assumed she'd been chasing after Babs. I knew that feeling only too well.

"Hi," she said, a little out of breath. "I thought I'd never catch her. Thank goodness she stopped to talk to your dog."

"Hi. Barry's just the same. If Babs hadn't come over to talk to him, he'd be long gone by now."

I was always a little cautious when I met new people in the park. I still had flashbacks to my run-in with Alicia when she'd tried to poison me ahead of the Levels competition. If it hadn't been for Grandma's quick action on that occasion, I would have been dead.

"I'm Dorothy," she said. "Do you live around here?"

"I live over Cuppy C; the cake shop and tea room."

"Oh yeah. I know it. The one run by the twins?"

"Yeah, they're my cousins."

"Ah! You must be Jill Gooder. You're a private investigator, aren't you?"

"That's me. I live in Washbridge most of the time. That's where my P.I. business is based. Over here, I just help out at Cuppy C occasionally to pay the rent."

"I've been thinking of moving to the human world," Dorothy said. "But, I'm beginning to have doubts."

"Why's that?"

"A few reasons, actually. I'd have to find a job, and of course somewhere to live. I don't know how easy that will be. I've worked in shops before, but only in Candlefield, so I'm not sure whether my skillset will be any good in the human world. And, I have no clue where to start looking for a flat. I don't suppose you could give me any pointers?"

"It's funny you should ask. I might be able to help."

"Really? That would be great."

"In fact, I might know someone who can help you with both the job and a flat."

"That would be absolutely fantastic. Who is it? Can I get in touch with them?"

"Before I give you their names, I need to speak to them first. Can you give me your contact details?"

She couldn't get her phone out quickly enough.

"I'll talk to them first, and if there is a job and or a flat going, I'll give you a call. In fact, I'll give you a call either way."

"That's great, Jill. Thanks very much. There is one other thing I'm a bit worried about."

"What's that?"

"I've never lived among humans. I'm just worried —"
She hesitated.

"Go on. Spit it out."

"I'm just worried that the temptation to feed off them might be too great."

"That's something you're definitely going to have to work on. The only reason there may be a flat and a job going is that the vampire you'd be replacing was brought back by the Rogue Retrievers for trying to do just that."

"Oh dear. Unlucky for them, but lucky for me, maybe. Anyway, if you would check and let me know, I'd be extremely grateful."

Chapter 13

Jack Maxwell caught up with me at the office a couple of days later.

"Just thought you'd want to know that we've charged Alison Shine with her sister's murder."

"And Tony Bow?"

"He's been released. Mind you, he said he'd rather stay locked up than have to face his wife." He grinned. "What put you onto Alison?"

"She's a bitter woman, but then you could hardly blame her—she has every right to be. She was the one who had to stay behind and look after their ailing father while Carly left home, got married, and started her own business. And, if Alison is to be believed, Carly never even asked how Alison was coping, and certainly never offered to help.

Alison became more and more resentful as the years went by, but what finally brought it to a head was when her dad told her that he intended to split their inheritance equally between the two sisters. You *could* argue that any parent would have done the same thing, but that would completely fail to acknowledge the sacrifice that Alison had made for him. Carly had a much better life—with money, and a business of her own. She didn't need help in the same way that Alison did.

The tipping point was when Carly told Alison about the publicity stunt that she and Gerry planned, and all the money they expected to make off the back of it. That caused something to snap inside of Alison. In her eyes, Carly already had far more money than she needed, and yet that still wasn't enough. Her sister's greed was too much for Alison to bear.

When Carly told Alison she didn't like the idea of hanging around in Black Woods, Alison saw her opportunity and said that she could hide out at her house. Carly didn't bother telling Gerry because she knew he'd object. While Carly was at her sister's, Alison gave her a drink laced with tranquilisers.

While Carly was out of it, Alison called the police, and told them that her brother-in-law had been in contact to tell her that her sister had gone missing. Then of course, she came to see me. She had to make sure she pointed the finger at Tony Bow, but she was very crafty in the way she did it. Initially, she focused on Gerry; she told me what a bad husband he was, which was of course a complete lie. Almost in passing, she mentioned that he'd accused Carly of having an affair with Tony Bow; something else which was blatantly untrue. But it was enough to sow a seed, and that was all she needed to do.

Tony Bow was a creature of habit, and a man who loved to have his car in showroom condition. He had it valeted on the same day every week at the car wash where Alison Shine worked. She knew exactly when he'd be coming in next, so it was easy for her to plant the necklace which she'd taken from Carly.

Then she put the final stage of her plan into action. Once Carly had come around enough so that she was able to walk, Alison told her there'd been a change of plan, and that Gerry wanted to meet her at the Bouncers office. That's where Alison killed her.

When I told Alison that Carly's body had been found, Alison put on one heck of an act. She didn't want to come right out and accuse Tony Bow; that would have been too obvious. Instead, she again pointed the finger at Gerry. She knew full well that I'd soon eliminate him from the enquiry, and hoped that at some point I'd recall her mentioning Tony Bow. Her plan worked like a dream.

When Tony Bow's wife gave me the necklace, I put two and two together and got five—just as Alison had hoped. That's when I brought you guys in."

"How come you didn't drop the case once Tony Bow had been arrested?" Maxwell said.

"I don't know. Instinct, I guess. I thought I might find more evidence in Tony Bow's car, and as it happened I did. But it wasn't the kind of evidence I'd expected. The air freshener had a picture of a whale on it. It was from the Moby Car Wash where Alison Shine worked.

Gerry Baxter had no reason to kill Carly. They were very much in love. Tony Bow had no reason to kill her either. Yes, he's a womaniser by all accounts, but he and Carly had never had any kind of relationship. Alison was the only one with a motive to kill her sister. She figured that with Carly gone, her dad would amend his Will and leave everything to her."

***

I'd had a rather mysterious phone call from Daze. She wanted to meet me in Cuppy C, but when I asked her what it was about, she didn't seem keen to discuss it on the phone.

I arrived in Candlefield with some time to spare, so I decided to drop in at Aunt Lucy's. As soon as I stepped inside, I could hear raised voices coming from the kitchen.

Aunt Lucy and Lester were both red in the face; it was obvious that they'd been arguing.

"I'm sorry if I've interrupted something."

"You aren't interrupting anything," Aunt Lucy said.

"Yes she is." Lester turned to me. "Jill, you know I'm not the sort of man to be unreasonable, am I?"

It was true. Lester was the most easy-going man I'd ever met. It was hard to imagine what could have made him so angry.

I just smiled; I didn't want to get in the middle of their argument.

"Tell her, Lucy. Tell her why I'm angry."

"You tell her if you want to." Aunt Lucy was obviously quite flustered.

"We've been trying to arrange our honeymoon," Lester said. "*Trying* being the operative word. Every time I come up with a suggestion, Lucy pooh-poohs it."

"I haven't *pooh-poohed* anything." Aunt Lucy sounded quite indignant. "I just said it wasn't somewhere I wanted to go."

"Yes. But you've said that to every suggestion I've made, and I must've come up with at least ten different options so far. They're either too hot or too expensive or too far away. It's been one excuse after another."

"They're not excuses. I'm sure we'll find somewhere we can both agree on."

"I've had enough of this." Lester stood up. "I'm sorry, Lucy, but I've tried my best. You decide where you want to go, and let me know." With that, he stormed out of the kitchen, slamming the door behind him.

Aunt Lucy looked a little down-hearted, but forced a smile. "I'm sorry you had to witness that. It's such a silly thing to argue over. There are so many places we could go to on honeymoon. I really don't know why we have to quarrel about it."

"Would you like me to make you a cup of tea?"

"That would be lovely, dear. And, I think we'll have some custard creams as well."

That sounded like my kind of plan.

***

When I arrived at Cuppy C, Daze was sitting at a window table with Mad. Much to my annoyance, they had taken the last two blueberry muffins.

"We've still got some chocolate muffins left," Pearl said.

"No thanks." I'd had my heart set on a blueberry one.

"Hi, Jill." Daze managed through a mouthful of muffin—*my muffin!*

Mad could only manage a nod; her mouth was so full of delicious blueberry muffin.

"Are you two enjoying those?"

"Mmm." Daze nodded.

"Delicious," Mad said, licking her lips.

"That's nice." I hope they choke you.

"Down to business," Daze said. "This may be our big chance to get TDO. We have some very good info."

"Are you sure we can rely on it?" I asked.

"You can never be one hundred percent sure of anything, but this is definitely the best intelligence we've had so far. According to our sources, TDO and Destro are going to meet in Washbridge."

"Why Washbridge? Isn't that asking for trouble?"

"Not really. They'll probably attract less attention there than if the meeting was to be held in Candlefield or Ghost Town."

"Don't you think we should inform Grandma or some of the other level six witches?"

"No." Daze was adamant. "They've had their chance. They've supposedly been trying to track down TDO for decades, and it's got them nowhere. I've long had my suspicions that they've been infiltrated at the very top level. Every time we get a tip-off, it seems to get back to TDO. We need to keep this between you, me and Mad. She's here because we need someone over in Ghost Town, and we know we can trust her."

"So what's the plan?"

"According to our sources, TDO and Destro plan to hammer out an agreement under which they can work together. If they manage to do that, then things are going to become very difficult for everyone in Candlefield and Ghost Town. The only thing we know for certain is that the meeting is being organised by none other than Ma Chivers."

My blood ran cold every time I thought of that woman. There was something about her; something really evil.

"In that case, I'll follow her so I can find out exactly when and where the meeting is going to be held." I volunteered.

"That's too dangerous." Daze shook her head. "I should be the one to do it."

"No!" I insisted. "If they spot you, it will destroy any chance we have of finding out where the meeting is to be held. But, if they were to spot me, I have the perfect excuse. Ma Chivers has been pestering me for some time now to let her take me under her wing. I'll tell her that I've changed my mind, and that I want her to tutor me."

"It's too risky," Daze said.

"No it's not. It's the only sensible way."

Mad nodded. "Jill's right, Daze. She's the only one of us who has a plausible reason for following Ma Chivers around. We have to let her do it."

"Okay." Daze agreed, but I could tell she still wasn't happy about it. "I'll give you a call when she's in Washbridge, and you can tail her."

***

While I was in Cuppy C, I went to check on Barry. He was exhausted; he'd just come back from a walk with the twins.

"Hi, Barry. How are you doing?"

"I'm tired. I'm going to sleep. I like to sleep. Do you like to sleep, Jill?"

"Yeah. When I'm tired."

"I love to sleep. Oh, by the way," Barry yawned. "Hamlet said he wanted to see you."

"Did he say why?"

"No." Barry's eyes were almost closed.

"Okay."

I walked down the corridor to the box room where I found Hamlet, glasses propped on the end of his nose, reading the rodent edition of Wuthering Heights.

"Not something I'd normally read," he said. "But not bad at all. Heathcliff is a nasty piece of work. Have you read it, Jill?"

"No, but I thought the song was good."

"Song?"

"Never mind. Barry said you wanted to see me."

"That's right. Thank you for dropping by. Look, I'll get

straight to the point." He put down his book, and moved across to the bars of the cage so that we were nose to nose. "You know that I'm now running a regular book club?"

"So I understand."

"Well, we've had the most astounding news."

"Really? What's that?"

"Horatio Moore has agreed to visit our club to give us a reading from his latest book. I can't tell you what an honour that is. I assume you're familiar with him?"

"Is he a footballer?"

Hamlet rolled his eyes in disgust. "No, Jill. He isn't a footballer. He's one of our leading contemporary authors."

"I can't say I've seen any of his books in the bookshop."

"He's not a human author. He's one of the most famous *hamster* authors of our day. It's a great honour that he has agreed to pay us a visit."

"I'm very pleased for you. I'm sure it'll be great."

"Yes, but look at this." He pointed to the cage.

"What about it?"

"Look at it. It's cheap. It's tacky."

"It cost me seventy-five pounds."

"It's altogether too small, and has no style. I can't possibly ask Horatio Moore to come and read to us in here."

"What do you expect me to do about it?"

"You'll have to buy a bigger one, of course. Something befitting of Horatio Moore."

"A new cage? You've only had this one five minutes."

"Would *you* invite a famous author to come and read in here?"

He had a point; it was a little on the small side. In my

defence, when I bought it, I hadn't anticipated that it would be used for a book club or for visiting famous authors.

"So, you want me to buy you a bigger cage?"

"Yes, but I'm not sure I can trust you to get it right. It's not just a question of buying a larger cage. It has to be stylish. It needs to have a certain je-ne-sais-quoi."

"I don't know what that means." I laughed at my own joke; Hamlet remained stony-faced.

"I'll have to come with you to the pet shop," Hamlet said. "That way, I can make sure you don't come back with any old tat."

"You want me to take you with me?"

"That's right. Any questions?"

"When did you want to do this?"

"I'm rather busy at the moment, but I'll give you a call when I'm free."

"That's very good of you."

"Okay. You may go now, Jill."

I had been dismissed.

Chapter 14

As soon as I walked into the office the next morning, I knew something was amiss. Mrs V was on her hands and knees on the floor, and there was yarn all around her.

"*He* did this," she said. "I'm going to kill him."

"*Who* did *what*?" I already knew the answer.

"That cat has stolen my yarn."

"Are you sure about that? You do have an awful lot of yarn."

"I'm absolutely positive. I bought six balls of midnight blue especially for my next project, and now there are only five in here."

"But Mrs V, you put a lock on the linen basket only last week because you said you were worried the Armitage people might help themselves to your yarn. How could Winky have got in there? Perhaps you miscounted them in the shop?"

She looked up, and fixed me with her gaze. She must have been taking lessons from Grandma.

"Or maybe you dropped one on the way back here?"

"I'm not stupid, Jill. I didn't miscount them, and I'm not in the habit of dropping balls of wool. I'm extremely careful when it comes to the transportation of yarn. That cat has taken it!"

"Even if Winky had somehow managed to get into the basket, he would have just emptied it all out, like he did when it was in the mail sack. Think about it. How could he undo the lock, steal just one ball, and then fasten the lock again?"

"I know he did it. I'm going to kill him."

"Look, I'll buy you another ball of—what colour did

you say it was?"

"Midnight blue."

"Okay, I'll buy you another ball of midnight blue wool."

"I still think it's that cat." She chuntered to herself.

I knew I wasn't going to change her mind, so I went through to my office.

"Winky, where are you?"

He crawled out from under my desk; he was obviously still half asleep.

"What's all the noise? I was having a fantastic dream. Cindy, Bella and me—"

"I don't want to hear about your sordid dreams."

"What's up with the old bag lady? She's been banging things around all morning."

"Have you stolen her wool?"

"What?" He scratched his nose.

"Mrs V's midnight blue wool. Have you stolen it?"

"Why would I want her wool?"

"I don't know. You might have done it just to spite her."

"No. I have *not* stolen her wool. Now, if you don't mind, I'd like to get back to my dream."

***

Why, oh why, did I volunteer for these things?

'Okay, Mrs V. I'll buy you a ball of midnight blue wool'.

Mrs V had failed to mention that midnight blue wool was about as rare as hen's teeth. I'd been trudging around Washbridge for the best part of two hours. I never realised there were so many small yarn shops. I'd started with Ever A Wool Moment, but Kathy had said I wouldn't find midnight blue for love nor money.

In every shop, I got the same response; they laughed in my face.

'Midnight blue? You won't find any of that.'

'Midnight blue? No chance!'

'Midnight blue? You're having a laugh!'

This was beginning to remind me of Christmas when I'd been trying to buy Total Dream Office for Lizzie. Winky had come to my rescue on that occasion, but I couldn't see him conjuring up a ball of midnight blue wool. Speaking of conjuring, what was the point of being a witch if I couldn't magic up a ball of wool?

If I returned empty handed, Mrs V would not be a happy camper. She needed six balls to finish her project — whatever *that* was. If I didn't find another ball of the stupid stuff, she'd have to abandon it, and then she'd probably kill me and Winky too.

I'd almost reached the point of giving up, when I stumbled across a tiny wool shop, tucked away in a corner of the market. It was so small that I hadn't noticed it before. It was called, *Where There's A Wool, There's A Way*. What was it with the crazy names for wool shops?

The woman behind the counter was all blue rinse and misery.

"What can I do for you?"

"I don't imagine you have a ball of midnight blue wool?"

"I might have."

"Is that a yes or a no?"

"Depends on what you're willing to pay."

"How much does it normally cost?"

"Five pounds, but it's the last one I've got. So, how much are you willing to pay?"

"I'll give you eight pounds for it."

"Fifty."

"Fifty? Are you having a laugh? For one ball of wool? That's extortionate."

"Take it or leave it."

"I'll give you ten."

She wiped her nose. "Forty."

"Twenty."

"Thirty."

"I'll give you twenty-five. Final offer."

"Done."

I had been—done up like a kipper.

While I was out and about in town, I popped into the fancy dress shop. It was much quieter than the last time I'd been in there. In fact, there was only one other customer in the shop; he was busy checking out the ghost outfits.

The two remaining owners were behind the counter, and I could see they remembered me as soon as I walked through the door.

"Hello again," the werewolf said. "I'm Charlie. We don't get many sups in here."

"I'm Jill. Nice to meet you."

"And I'm Neil." The wizard offered his hand. "Are you looking for anything in particular?"

"I understand the young vampire who served me last time has left the business."

I didn't think it would go down well if I let them know I'd been instrumental in getting her arrested and taken back to Candlefield by Daze.

"Ruth? Yeah, we'd warned her numerous times that the Rogue Retrievers would catch up with her sooner or later, but she wouldn't listen."

"I guess that means you're short of one member of staff, and presumably you're a flatmate short as well?"

"That's right. Ruthie dropped us right in it. When it's quiet like today, the two of us can easily run the shop, but you've seen how busy it can get. At the weekend, it can be quite manic, so we're definitely going to have to find someone to work in the shop. And yeah, we need a new flatmate as well. We share a loft; it's huge and a great place to live, but we could barely afford the rent between three of us. Two of us certainly can't manage to pay it. Ideally we need another two to share, but it isn't easy to find sup flatmates."

"Actually, that's the reason I called in today."

"Are you looking for a job or a flat?"

"Me? Neither. But I know a sup who is looking for both. When I was in the park in Candlefield recently, I bumped into a young female vampire who told me that she was hoping to move to Washbridge. She needs a job and somewhere to live, so I thought of you guys. I didn't tell her who you are or make her any promises, other than to say I would ask to see what you thought. She did say that she's had experience of working in shops."

"I don't know," Charlie said. "After the experience with Ruth, I'm not sure we want another vampire. They just can't control themselves. As soon as they see a human neck, the fangs are out."

"I understand what you're saying, but how else are you going to find a sup who is a ready-made shop assistant and a flatmate?"

"That's true," Neil said. "We should at least talk to her. What's her name?"

"Dorothy. Look, if you think it's worthwhile, I can get her to come in and see you. Then you can decide whether you like the look of her. If you don't, nothing lost, but if you do, it will have saved you a lot of time and energy."

"Okay then. Tell Dorothy to get in touch with us," Charlie said. "We'll have a chat with her, and take it from there."

I took the stupid midnight blue wool back to the office.

"How much do I owe you, dear?" Mrs V was all smiles now.

"Err—I—err."

"It's usually five pounds. I hope you didn't pay over the odds."

"Five pounds? That's right. That's exactly what I paid."

She checked her purse. "I've only got two pounds-fifty with me. I can let you have the rest tomorrow."

"You know what? It doesn't matter. I'll knock it off your wages."

***

I received a call from Hamlet; he was now ready to look at cages, so I magicked myself over to Candlefield. Barry was out with the twins when I went upstairs to collect my well-read hamster from the box room.

We made our way over to Rupert's Pets; the shop where I'd bought Hamlet.

"Is Eddie in today?"

"No, he's on holiday. I'm Rupert, can I help?" He glanced at the cage in my hand. "Did you buy that hamster here?"

"I did."

"Is there a problem with it?"

"No. No problem. It's just that we're going to need a bigger cage."

Rupert glanced again at the cage. "It looks like there's plenty of room in there to me."

"There is. It's just that Hamlet has started a book club."

"I see. So many of our hamsters do. Rodent edition books are a big part of our business these days. I assume he needs a bigger cage to accommodate the members of the club?"

"Not just that. Apparently he has—"

"I can speak for myself," Hamlet said.

"Sorry."

"Horatio Moore is coming to read for us. You may have heard of him?"

"Of course," Rupert said. "You're very honoured. I understand he's very much in demand."

I felt a bit left out of the conversation.

"So anyway," Hamlet continued. "I can't possibly expect Horatio Moore to give a reading in this *thing*. I'm going to need your very best, top of the range cage. Something that royalty would be proud to visit."

"Of course. You'll need the Elite Range."

"Just a minute," I interrupted. "Elite Range? That sounds expensive."

"Money is no object," Hamlet said.

"Whoa! Hang on. Money is most definitely an object if it's *my* money. Don't you have any money?"

"Why would I have money? I'm a hamster."

"Can't you charge your members a fee to attend the reading?"

"That would be tacky. Come on, Jill, we don't have all day. Let's take a look at these cages."

Rupert led us across the shop to an area with an illuminated sign, which read: *The Elite Range*. The cages there were truly spectacular; far bigger and much more handsome than the one which Hamlet currently had. I tried to see how much they cost, but there didn't appear to be any price tickets on them.

"How much are these, exactly?"

"This is the Elite One. It's one hundred pounds."

"I suppose I could run to that."

"No," Hamlet said. "That one won't do."

"Then we have the Elite Two. That is one hundred and fifty pounds."

"One hundred and fifty pounds? I suppose I could —"

"We can't expect Horatio Moore to spend time in there."

"And the top of the range is the Elite Three. As you can see, this one has everything a hamster could possibly require. The metalwork has been hand-crafted. Look at the ornate detailing on the top. It's absolutely beautiful."

"How much is that?" I hardly dared to ask.

"That one is two hundred and twenty-five pounds."

"Two hundred and — ?"

"We'll take it," Hamlet said. "That's just what we need. I'm sure Horatio will be happy to do a reading in there."

"But it's two hundred and twenty-five pounds!"

"Plus tax," Rupert said.

Chapter 15

I'd spotted Betty Longbottom in the distance. I wanted a word with that little madam.

"Betty!"

"Sorry, Jill. Got to dash."

"Betty wait!"

When I caught up with her, I could tell by the worried look on her face that she knew exactly why I wanted to speak to her.

"Have you taken them back?" I said, still trying to catch my breath.

"Taken what back?"

"You know what I mean. All the contraband you had squirrelled away in your flat."

"Most of it."

"How much is 'most of it'?"

"The lion's share."

"So can I take a look in your spare bedroom tonight?"

"There's no need for that, Jill. Don't you trust me?"

"In a word, *no*. Come on, Betty, I want to know. How much have you taken back?"

"Two handbags and some shoes."

"How many shoes?"

"Two."

"Two pairs?"

"No. Two shoes — one pair."

"At this rate, it will take you over a decade to take everything back."

"But it took so long to collect them."

"You didn't *collect* them; you *stole* them. Now either you take everything back or I have a word with my friend the detective."

"Don't do that, Jill, please."

"Okay, but you have to do it this time. Promise?"

"I promise."

I felt a little bad for being so hard on her, so I tried to lighten the conversation. "Are you seeing anyone at the moment?"

Her face lit up. "It's funny you should mention that because I am as it happens. And I think this one may be a keeper."

"Really?"

She laughed. "Only kidding. His name is Keeper."

Oh dear! It couldn't be, could it?

"Jim works some very strange hours, and always seems to be on call. He's very sweet though."

Sweet? Jim Keeper the grim reaper?

"What does he do?"

"I don't know for sure. I've tried asking him a couple of times, but he changes the subject. Mind you, I think I've worked it out."

This should be interesting.

"I think he's an undertaker because he always dresses in black. That's probably why he won't tell me. He probably thinks it would put me off."

"Yeah, that must be it."

"He didn't even freak out when I told him about my sea-shell collection. And, it turns out that he has a collection of his own which is even more unusual than mine."

"What does Jim collect?" Lost souls?

"Scythes. Apparently, he has a whole room full of them. He said I should go over to his place to see them sometime. He did tell me where he lives, but I forget now."

Hades?

***

Amber and Pearl had an appointment with their bank manager, and had left me in charge of the shop for an hour. I didn't mind stepping in for short periods just so long as they didn't try to pull another 'Premier Day' stunt. Thankfully, it was fairly quiet, and I was coping quite nicely. I had a couple of assistants with me in case I got into any difficulty, but so far so good.

The door opened, and in walked two familiar faces: Miles Best and his girlfriend, Mindy. They were our competition in the form of Best Cakes who were located across the road from Cuppy C. What could they possibly want?

"Morning, Miles," I said. "Morning, Mindy. I'm rather surprised to see you two in here."

"We thought it was time to bury the hatchet," Miles said. "Call a truce, so to speak. I realise that we're partly at fault for the animosity."

"Partly?"

"Maybe we let our competitive streak get the better of us. Anyway, we're here now to offer an olive branch. Hopefully we can make a fresh start."

"The twins aren't here at the moment. You really ought to be talking to them. It is their shop after all."

"Have we missed them?" Miles looked disappointed. "That's rather unfortunate timing. Perhaps you'll convey our message of conciliation?"

"Of course. Would you like a drink while you're here?"

"Why not? Always good to check out the competition." He laughed. "I'll have a latte, please."

"What about you, Mindy?"

"I'll have the same. A caramel one, please, Jill. By the way, did I see you with a dog the other day?"

"Yes. That's Barry, my Labradoodle."

"I love dogs. Labradoodles in particular. I don't suppose he's here now is he?"

"He's upstairs in the flat."

"Could I see him?"

"I can't really leave the shop."

"Maybe I could pop upstairs, and say hello to him?"

"I suppose that wouldn't do any harm. But he's very excitable, so be careful he doesn't knock you over."

"It's okay. I've been around dogs all my life. I'm sure I can handle him."

Mindy disappeared upstairs to the flat, leaving Miles and I to make small talk.

A few minutes later, she re-joined us. I couldn't figure out what had prompted this. Ever since they'd opened Best Cakes, they'd been very competitive, and had even resorted to sabotage. Now, suddenly out of the blue, they wanted to be friends? Something just didn't feel right. But it wasn't my problem. That was something for the twins to sort out with them. After they'd finished their drinks, Miles and Mindy said goodbye, and walked back across the road to Best Cakes.

A few minutes later, there was an ear piercing scream, and the woman at the table next to the window jumped up onto her chair. Seconds later, another woman in the corner seat screamed; she too climbed onto her chair.

What was going on?

"There's a mouse!" the first woman screamed.

"That's not a mouse," the man sitting next to her said. "That's a rat."

Suddenly someone else screamed, "Rats!"

I came out from behind the counter, and sure enough, there on the floor were three rats scurrying back and forth. Two women were screaming; one of the men was screaming too. Slowly but surely everyone made their way out of the shop — some of them stepping from one chair to the next.

Just as the last few customers were leaving, Amber and Pearl returned.

"What's going on, Jill? Why is everybody leaving?"

"We've got rats," I said. "Look! Over there!"

The twins stared in disbelief. "Where did *they* come from? We've never had rats before."

"I've no idea. I just—" Then, a little bell rang in my head. "It must have been Miles."

"Miles?" Amber looked puzzled. "What does he have to do with it?"

"He and Mindy came over a while ago. He said that he wanted to offer an olive branch — to make a new start."

"How did he manage to get the rats in here?"

"That must have been Mindy. She had a bag with her when she went upstairs. At least, I thought she'd gone upstairs."

"Why did you let her go up there, Jill?"

"She said she wanted to say hello to Barry. She must have sneaked around the back, and let the rats out of her bag."

"I'm going to kill him!" Pearl started for the door.

"Not if I get to him first," Amber said.

I put myself in between them and the door. "You can't do that. You'll get arrested."

"But look what he's done. If word gets around that we've got rats, we'll be finished."

"That won't happen. There were only a few people in here. You're more likely to attract attention if you go over there and cause a fuss."

"We're not going to let this lie," Amber said. "We'll have our revenge."

"Yes." Pearl thumped the counter. "We'll make him suffer for this."

The twins called in a friend of theirs who used to work for a pest control company. He made short work of rounding up the rats—I didn't ask what he intended to do with them—sometimes ignorance is bliss.

To try to take the twins' minds off the rat infestation, I changed the subject.

"Aunt Lucy and Lester were having a right go at each other when I was around there the other day."

"What about?" Amber said.

"Their honeymoon. Lester keeps suggesting places they could go, but Aunt Lucy shoots them all down in flames. He's getting tired of it. She either says it's too expensive or too hot or too—"

"That's not why she doesn't want to go," Pearl said.

"What do you mean?"

"Mum's scared of flying."

"Really?"

"Scared of aeroplanes to be precise. She's only ever been on one; it turned her into a nervous wreck. Ever since then, she's refused to fly."

"If that's the reason, why doesn't she just tell Lester?"

"She doesn't like to admit it. I think she's embarrassed," Pearl said. "It's stupid really. It would be far easier just to tell him than to let him keep coming up with destinations when she knows that she's going to say no anyway."

"He stormed out while I was there."

"Oh, dear. Do you think the wedding's off?" Amber said.

"It had better not be," Pearl chimed in. "I want to be a bridesmaid."

"Perhaps I should have a word with Lester?" I suggested. "I could tell him about Aunt Lucy's fear of flying."

"Don't tell him we told you. Mum will kill us."

"I'll be discreet."

The twins rolled their eyes.

"What? I can be discreet. I'll take him to one side and let him know what's what, and then, hopefully, he'll come up with somewhere that doesn't involve aeroplanes."

***

Even though Charlie and Neil at the fancy dress shop had said they were willing to give Dorothy a chance, I was beginning to have second thoughts. Should I really be getting involved? What did I actually know about Dorothy? Nothing more than what she'd told me in our brief conversation.

I decided to trust it to fate. I'd take Barry to the park, and if I bumped into Dorothy again, I would take that as a sign that I should tell her about the flat and the job. But if she wasn't there, then I'd let sleeping dogs lie.

Scientific eh?

"Do you want to go to the park, Barry?"

"Yes, please. I love going to the park. Can we go for a walk?"

"That's why we're going to the park."

"I love to go for walks."

"I know you do, Barry. Come on, then. Let's go."

"Will Babs be there?"

"I don't know. Maybe."

"I hope so. I like Babs. She likes to go to the park too."

"So I hear."

"And she likes to go for a walk."

It never got any easier.

We'd been in the park for the best part of an hour, and there'd been no sign of Dorothy or Babs. Obviously, the fates had decided I should let it lie. It was probably for the best.

"Come on, then, Barry. Let's go home."

As always, he ignored me, and carried on running around the park like a crazy dog. I didn't have the energy to chase after him, but figured a few treats might do the job.

"Barry! Look what I've got. Barkies! Come and get them!"

Barry started to run towards me, but then suddenly stopped dead in his tracks. What was going on? He never hesitated when treats were involved. Then suddenly, he ran in the opposite direction. I never thought I'd see the day when Barry turned his nose up at treats, but then I spotted Dorothy and Babs.

"Hello there, Jill." Dorothy let Babs off the lead, and the two dogs began to chase one another around the park.

"Hi. You nearly missed us. We were just about to go home. Barry actually turned his nose up at a treat when he spotted Babs. He never does that."

"They seem very fond of each other, don't they?"

Barry and Babs were still running wild, up and down the park. If only I had a quarter of their energy.

"Did you manage to ask your friends about the job and the flat?"

"Yes. They said that they'd be happy to talk to you about both."

"Really? That's fantastic."

"I can't promise anything. It's obviously their decision, but if you're still interested — ?"

"I'm definitely interested. I'm so grateful, Jill."

"Not a problem." I gave her the name and address of the shop.

"I'd really like to do something by way of a thank you. Perhaps, we could go out in Washbridge some time? My treat. Maybe have a night out or a coffee or something?"

Memories of my meeting with Alicia came flooding back.

"Yeah, probably. Why don't you get your job and flat sorted out first, and then we can take it from there?"

Chapter 16

I popped into Aunt Lucy's, and managed to catch Lester on his own in the living room.

"Lester," I said in a whisper. "Can I have a word?"

"What is it, Jill?"

"I think I know why Aunt Lucy is being so difficult over the honeymoon."

"That woman is driving me crazy."

"You mustn't let her know that I've told you, but she's scared of aeroplanes."

"She never said."

"She's embarrassed to admit it. Maybe you could come up with somewhere that doesn't involve travelling on an aeroplane? Maybe a nice railway journey or a cruise, if you can afford it?"

"Thanks for telling me, Jill. She should have said something."

"You won't tell her I told you, will you?"

"Mum's the word. I'll do some research, and see if I can come up with some ideas. Thanks again, Jill."

"No problem."

Just then, I heard voices in the kitchen.

"Your grandmother is in there with Lucy. You're in for a surprise when you see her."

"How do you mean?"

"You'll see." Lester grinned, and before I could ask him any more questions, he disappeared out of the door.

Grandma and surprises were not a good combination, but curiosity got the better of me. She and Aunt Lucy were seated at the kitchen table.

"Hi, Jill," Aunt Lucy said.

"Hello, Jill." Grandma smiled at me. "Would you like a cup of tea? I'll make it."

Something was definitely not right. I had to sit down before I fell down. What was going on? Grandma had just smiled *and* offered to make tea. I looked to Aunt Lucy for an explanation, but she just grinned.

"How many sugars is it, Jill?" Grandma asked.

"One and two thirds, please."

"No problem."

No problem? Normally, *everything* was a problem to Grandma.

After placing the tea on the table in front of me, she offered me custard creams.

"Thanks. I'll just have one. Or two. Or maybe three, thanks."

"Three it is. Well I have work to do, so I'll shoot off. Have a lovely day both of you." With that, Grandma, or whoever this imposter was, left.

I don't think I'd ever been so stunned. I stared at the cup of tea, and wondered if I dare drink it.

"What's going on, Aunt Lucy? Has Grandma put something in this tea?"

"No. It's perfectly safe." She laughed.

"But what's happening?"

"You're never going to believe this, but an old flame of your grandma's has turned up—his name is Horace. He and Grandma were an *item* ages ago, but then he more or less disappeared off the face of the earth. He's been in the human world, apparently. Anyway, he's back now, and he's asked Grandma out on a date."

"Grandma? On a date? Wow!"

***

I was helping out behind the counter in Cuppy C again, and the twins were acting very suspiciously.

Every now and then, they would huddle together, talk in a whisper, and then laugh out loud. Were they talking about me or was I just being paranoid? Either way, I was going to have it out with them.

"Amber, Pearl, do you have a minute?"

"Sure," Amber said. "What's up?

"What are you up to?"

"Who? Us?" They both put on their innocent look.

"Yes, you two. Come on, I know something's going on. Are you talking about me?"

"Why would you think we're talking about you?" Pearl said.

"Because you're whispering. You obviously don't want me to hear what you're saying."

"If you must know, we were talking about Grandma."

"What about her?"

"If we tell you, we'll have to swear you to secrecy."

How very cloak and dagger. Now, I was really intrigued. "I won't tell her. What are you up to?"

"You've heard about her old flame, haven't you?"

"Horace? Yeah. Who'd have thought it? He must be something really special if he's managed to bring a smile to Grandma's face."

"We're going to spy on her when she has her first date with him," Pearl whispered.

"Are you two *insane*?"

"It'll be fun," Amber said. "Can you imagine seeing Grandma with a man? It'll be hilarious."

"It won't be hilarious when she catches you."

"She won't catch us."

"Of course she will. She knows everything that we do—sometimes before we do it. You've got a short memory. Don't you remember what she did to you the last time you played a trick on her?"

Both girls touched their ears, no doubt remembering when Grandma had turned them into donkey's ears.

"It'll be different this time," Amber said. "We'll be more careful."

"Yeah," Pearl agreed. "We've got it all planned out. We'll be super careful. If you want to come with us, you can."

"Definitely not. I don't have a death-wish even if you two do."

"It'll be fun. Come on. Don't you want to see her snogging Horace?"

Just the thought of it turned my stomach. "No, I don't. And especially not if it means having donkey's ears for the rest of my life. You two are on your own. Just don't come crying to me when she casts a spell on you."

I'd been hard at it behind the counter for almost two hours.

"Hey, girls. I think it's time I had a break, don't you?"

"Okay, go on, Jill," Pearl said. "You can have ten minutes."

The twins were still busy plotting their ill-fated spying expedition. I was having no part of it. Would they never learn?

I grabbed a blueberry muffin and a latte, and found myself a seat next to the window. I'd only been there a few minutes when Blaze came through the door; it was unusual to see him without Daze. He spotted me and came over.

"Where's Daze? Is she okay?"

"Yeah, she's fine. I just sneaked away for a few minutes." He glanced around as though he thought someone might be listening.

"Is everything okay?" I asked.

"Yeah. Look, there's something I want to run by you, but I'm going to have to swear you to secrecy first."

What was with all the subterfuge all of a sudden?

"I promise I won't say anything."

"Yesterday, I was offered a job by another Rogue Retriever. Her name is Taze."

"Taze? Wow! So that's Daze, Haze, Blaze, and now Taze."

"Yeah, quite a coincidence, isn't it? She needs a new sidekick. Her previous partner quit to go and work in the bottling factory."

"Quite the change of career."

"Taze said she'd heard good things about me. She's offering more money than Daze pays me, and more importantly, she's promised that I can have my choice of catsuit; any colour I like—even luminous."

"You must be flattered."

"I am. Very much so."

"Are you going to take her up on the offer?"

"I'm torn. Daze has been very good to me, and I like her a lot, but she's a bit bossy. You know how she can be, Jill."

It was true. Daze was very set in her ways, particularly when it came to colours. I'd seen her tear a strip off Blaze for wearing a luminous orange catsuit.

"So, what do you think, Jill?"

"I'm sorry, Blaze, but this is something you're going to have to decide for yourself."

"I know, I know. It's a difficult decision, though. I think I'm going to have to sleep on it. You won't mention this to Daze, will you?"

"No, of course not. I promise."

"And don't tell the twins because you know what they're like. They can't keep a secret."

That was true enough.

"My lips are sealed. I won't tell anyone, but you must let me know what you decide."

***

It suddenly occurred to me that today was the day Hamlet was expecting his visiting author, Horatio Moore. So, seeing as I'd spent so much money on the new cage, I figured I should call in on them to see what all the fuss was about.

I made my way to the box room, and opened the door as quietly as I could. I didn't want to disturb a genius at work.

"Jill," Hamlet said. "Is that you?"

"I hope you don't mind me popping in. I thought I might listen to Horatio's reading."

"You've missed him, I'm afraid. He just left."

"How disappointing."

"He was very good wasn't he?" Hamlet addressed the audience. There were at least fifteen hamsters in the cage. They all nodded their approval.

"If I'd realised, I would have come earlier."

"All is not lost," Hamlet said. "Horatio did leave behind a few signed copies of his latest hardback — rodent edition of course."

"Of course."

"Perhaps you'd like a copy?"

I'd paid for the cage, so why not? At least I would have got something out of the deal. It might be a little bit hard to read because the rodent edition hardback was rather small, but I could always use a magnifying glass.

"That would be very nice, thank you."

Hamlet passed the tiny book through the bars of the cage. I opened it and sure enough, there was the signature. I was the proud owner of a signed edition of Horatio Moore's latest novel.

"That'll be thirty-five pounds please, Jill," Hamlet said.

"Pardon?"

"For the book. We've agreed to send the proceeds onto Horatio. The regular copy is only twenty, but a signed copy is thirty-five."

"Thirty-five pounds?"

"A bargain, isn't it?"

"An absolute steal."

***

Back in my office, I was still trying to get my head around the idea of Grandma going on a date with an old flame. Horace, the new man in her life, certainly seemed to have changed her personality for the better — I wondered how long that would last.

I was trying hard to concentrate on the papers in front of me, but I could barely hear myself think. Winky was on the treadmill again, and seemed to be going faster than ever. His iPod was clipped to the belt around his waist; he had his headphones on, and he was singing at the top of his voice. That cat could not carry a tune—trust me on that one. I thought Betty Longbottom had a horrible voice, but I would take Betty any day of the week over Winky. I couldn't even tell *what* he was singing, but whatever it was, he was murdering it.

"Shut up!" I shouted.

He was oblivious. He just kept on running, and singing.

"Stop singing!"

It was hopeless; he was in a world of his own.

It was just too much to bear. I thumped on the desk as hard as I could, and suddenly, a small drawer at the bottom shot open. My father had had the desk for as long as he'd had the office; it was something of an antique. But I'd had absolutely no idea there were hidden drawers in it.

I crouched down, and managed to slide my hand inside to grab hold of the contents, which I dropped onto the desk. A ball of wool? It couldn't be, could it? I checked the label: midnight blue. The only other items in the drawer were a few small tools.

Then it clicked.

Lock-picking tools! Winky must have used them to get into the linen basket. He *had* stolen Mrs V's wool! I was going to kill him!

"What do you call these?" I screamed, but he still couldn't hear a thing.

Right! I'd had just about enough. I got up from my desk, walked over to the power socket, and turned off the switch. The treadmill stopped dead—but Winky didn't.

He flew straight across the room, bounced off the leather sofa, and came to rest on the floor.

"What are you playing at," he said, pulling the earphones off. "You nearly killed me!"

I held up the wool and the lock-picking tools. "What do you call these?"

"Whoops!" He looked a little sheepish. "You found them."

"Yes, I found them."

"Sorry about that. Just my little joke."

"I'm going to kill you, Winky."

He shot under the sofa. Probably just as well or I might have done something I would have regretted later.

I waited until I heard Mrs V pop out to the loo, then called, "Winky, if you don't want me to kill you, come with me now."

He knew I meant business, so he followed me through to the outer office.

"Open this lock, quickly."

I passed him the lock-picking tools, and within seconds he had it open. I dropped the wool inside, and then slammed the linen basket shut, and fastened the lock.

"Give me those tools back," I demanded.

"But they're mine." He backed off.

"Give them to me or you'll never have salmon again."

"You're such a spoilsport." He handed over the tools.

"Get back in my office. I don't want to hear another word from you all day."

"Can't I go on the treadmill?"

"That's going back to the shop. Today!"

Chapter 17

The next morning, Mrs V was red in the face, and breathing fire. Something had got her really riled up.

"Whatever is wrong, Mrs V?"

"I'm going to kill him."

She must have somehow worked out what had happened with the midnight blue wool.

"I'm sure Winky didn't mean any harm."

"Not the cat. That reporter, Dougal Bugle."

"Has he been here?"

"No, and it's a good thing for him he hasn't or he'd have one of my knitting needles up his backside."

"What has he done?"

"Look at this!" She thumped the newspaper which was on her desk.

It was the headline that Dougal had warned me he would print. *Slavery alive and well in Washbridge.*

"How dare he publish that without at least speaking to me first?" She fumed. "I'm nobody's slave. I come here because I choose to. I'm well aware that I spend most of the time knitting, but I don't feel guilty about it because that's the arrangement you and I have. This is no one's business other than ours. Did you know he was going to do this, Jill?"

There was no point in lying.

"He doorstepped me the other day, and suggested that he might run the article."

"And, you didn't think you should tell me?"

"I thought I'd persuaded him to drop it. I explained what our arrangement was, and that you did it voluntarily. I also told him you spend a considerable amount of time knitting."

"You should have told me, Jill. I had a right to know."

"You're right. I'm really sorry. But it's Dougal that we should both be angry at."

"Don't worry, dear. I know who's fault this is, and when I get hold of him, I'll make him regret the day he ever put pen to paper."

"Where do you think he got the story from, anyway?" I said. "How would *he* know that you don't get paid? It's not like we broadcast it. I mean, Kathy and one or two other people know, but no one who would take it to The Bugle."

"Come on, Jill. You're supposed to be the private investigator. Even I know where he got the story from."

I scratched my chin. I was probably being a little slow. But then the penny dropped.

"Armitage."

"Of course it's Armitage. Who else? I may have made the mistake of mentioning it to some of his staff who come around here for knitting lessons. But only in a jokey kind of way. I wasn't complaining. You know me—I'm perfectly happy with our arrangement."

"And you think one of them might have told Gordon Armitage?"

"It's possible. I doubt they would have done it maliciously. Perhaps they were talking amongst themselves, and he overheard?"

Mrs V was right. My money was on Armitage.

"There's nothing we can do about it now," I said. "We'll just have to forget about it. It'll be tomorrow's fish and chip paper."

"*You* might be prepared to forget about it, but *I'm*

certainly not. Dougal Andrews and Gordon Armitage have a lot to answer for."

***

My phone rang; it was Daze.

"Ma Chivers is in Washbridge right now. She's been seen close to the bus station."

"Okay. I'll get over there straight away."

"I still think I should be the one to follow her, Jill."

"No, I've got this. I'll call you if I need any help."

"Just be careful."

Ma Chivers wasn't difficult to spot. She was the biggest and ugliest woman in the vicinity. I followed her at a distance, and when she entered the Fleur Hotel, I gave her a few seconds and then did likewise. She took the lift, so I cast the 'faster' spell, and headed straight for the staircase. On each level, I checked to see if she'd got out of the lift. On the seventh floor, she did. At the end of the corridor, she took a right. I set off in pursuit, but then suddenly the door to one of the rooms on my right, flew open in front of me.

"What are you doing here?" a familiar, but unwelcome, voice said.

It was Alicia, and next to her, as though joined at the hip, was Cyril.

"I — err — want to speak to Ma Chivers."

"That's *Mrs* Chivers to you," Alicia spat the words. "Why do you want to speak to her?"

"I've had a change of heart. I want to take her up on her offer to tutor me."

"I don't believe you. You're a liar!"

"Whereas you, of course, are as honest as the day is long? Particularly when you're poisoning someone?"

"You've made one mistake too many, Gooder. You're not going to see Ma Chivers. In fact, you're not going to see tomorrow." She raised her hand, and I knew she was about to cast a spell.

"What are you doing?" A voice boomed from the end of the corridor. Ma Chivers must have heard us.

"Gooder says she's changed her mind," Alicia said. "She reckons she wants to study under you. I don't trust her."

"Me neither," Cyril said.

Ma Chivers looked me up and down, and I could almost feel the heat from her eyes burning into me. I was trying to hold it together; trying not to show how scared I felt. If she realised what I was actually doing there, I was a dead woman.

"I thought you wanted nothing to do with me," she said. "I've asked you twice, and both times you've turned me down. Why the change of heart?"

"I've had time to think about it. I want to be the best witch I can be, and I believe my best chance of achieving that is under your guidance."

"What about your grandmother? What does she have to say about it?"

"I haven't told her yet."

"Why doesn't that surprise me?"

"I love Grandma, but I have to admit that she seems a little distracted at the moment. She's been very involved with her commercial enterprise in the human world."

"You mean that stupid wool shop of hers?"

"Yeah. She also stood for the town council, which took up a lot of her time."

"Came a close second, I heard?" Ma Chivers sneered.

"Anyway, like I said, I want to be taught by the best, and I figure that's you." I almost choked on my own words, but I had to make it convincing.

Ma Chivers seemed quite pleased by that. Not only was she evil, but she was also vain. That might work in my favour. It meant there was a slim chance I might get away with this.

"If you're going to come under my wing, you should know that I'm very demanding, and I'm also mean. Very mean. Isn't that right, Alicia?"

Alicia nodded.

"And I'll expect quid pro quo. You'll get the best possible tuition, but in return I'll ask you to do me the odd favour. And, you may not always find those favours palatable. But I'll expect you to carry them out, anyway. It's all part of proving your loyalty to me. Do you understand?"

"Yes. I understand." I was beginning to think I'd pulled it off. She seemed to be warming to the idea, although I could tell that Alicia still wasn't convinced.

Just then, a smartly dressed man came walking towards us. "I need a few words about the conference room you've booked, madam."

"Jill, you've made the right decision." Ma Chivers put her grubby hand on my shoulder—I felt dirty. "Now, will you excuse me for a moment?"

She and the smartly dressed man went into the room from which Alicia and Cyril had emerged.

"I still don't trust you, Gooder," Alicia said.

"I don't think it's up to you." I was only half listening to her because I'd cast a spell so that I could overhear the conversation inside the room.

Sure enough, moments later, I had all the information I needed.

Once outside, I made a call to Daze.

"Are you okay, Jill?" She sounded concerned.

"Yeah, I'm fine, but not quite everything went according to plan."

"How do you mean? You're not hurt, are you?"

"No, nothing like that. I followed Ma Chivers to the Fleur Hotel, but I ran into Alicia and Cyril. I think I might have got away with it though. Like we agreed, I told Ma Chivers that I'd had a change of heart, and wanted to work under her."

"Did she buy it?"

"It's hard to tell, but I think so. I don't think I would have got out of there in one piece otherwise. The important thing is I know when the meeting is taking place. It's tomorrow at two pm in a conference room on the seventh floor of the Fleur Hotel."

"Well done, Jill! We've got him now. We've got TDO at last!"

***

I could hear the commotion as soon as I walked into the building. There, on the landing was Mrs V. She had Gordon Armitage pinned against the wall, and she was brandishing a knitting needle. The poor man looked absolutely terrified. *Poor man*? Who was I kidding? What did *I* care about Gordon Armitage? Part of me hoped she'd just stick the needle in his throat and have done with it.

"Mrs V," I shouted, but she was so enraged that she was oblivious to my presence.

"How dare you spread rumours about me," she screamed at Armitage.

"I have no idea what you're talking about."

"You know very well what I'm talking about." Mrs V moved the knitting needle even closer to his jugular. "The article in The Bugle. You're responsible for this, aren't you?"

"I only told them the truth."

"You wouldn't know the truth if it came and slapped you around the face. Jill, and her father before her, have been like family to me. It's true—she doesn't pay me, but that doesn't make me a slave. She told me that she couldn't keep me on after her father died because there wasn't enough money in the business, but I insisted I wanted to carry on working here anyway because I love it. It's not as though I do much work anyway. Goodness knows you spend enough time in our office—have you ever been in there when I wasn't knitting?"

He couldn't speak because he was too focused on the knitting needle which was now only inches from his eye.

"If I didn't come to work, I'd be sat at home by myself. Jill is actually doing me a favour, and I really cannot see what business it is of yours whether she pays me or not."

I had to intervene before Mrs V did something she'd regret, so I walked up behind her, and grabbed her arm.

"Leave me alone, Jill. Let me stab him."

"No, Mrs V. Don't give him the satisfaction."

Reluctantly, she let him go.

Armitage was still red in the face, but tried to compose himself. "You've done it now," he said. "That was assault. Now I have a real story to tell The Bugle. And I'm sure the police will want to hear about this too. You'll be arrested within the hour." He glared at Mrs V who seemed totally unconcerned by his rantings.

"Go back into the office, Mrs V. I'll handle this."

"Can't I just stab him once?" she pleaded.

"No. Leave it to me. I'll sort this out."

Reluctantly, she left me to it.

"You're finished, Gooder," Armitage said. "You'll be out by the end of the week!"

I cast the 'forget' spell.

"What's going on?" He looked confused. "Why am I out here?"

"I've no idea, Gordon. I heard a noise, and came out to check. Did you fall?"

"I don't know. Perhaps I did. I don't remember."

"I should lay off the drink if I was you, Gordon."

Chapter 18

The next day, I was as nervous as I'd ever been in my life. I'd arranged to meet Daze and Mad in Cuppy C ahead of our assault on TDO in Washbridge.

I could see the twins were stressed out as soon as I walked through the door.

"What's up, girls?"

"Don't ask," Pearl said.

"I just did."

"We have some unwelcome visitors." Amber frowned.

"Don't tell me you have rats again."

"Not exactly, although I suppose you could call them rats." Pearl spoke in a low voice. "They're in the back."

"Who's in the back?"

"The hygiene inspectors."

"Hygiene—"

"Shh! Don't let them hear you."

"Why are they here?"

"Why do you think? Somebody tipped them off about the rats."

"Who would do that?"

"Can't you guess?"

"Miles?"

"Who else?"

"Excuse me." A man wearing metal rimmed glasses appeared from the back of the shop. "Who's in charge here?"

"I am," Amber said.

"I am," Pearl echoed.

He looked from one to the other.

"We both are. We're joint owners."

"Would you come through to the back? I want to show you something."

Amber and Pearl both looked really worried as they followed him. I tagged along behind.

"Look there." He pointed to something on the floor.

"I can't see anything." Amber screwed up her eyes.

"That's a dropping of some kind." He pointed again.

"No, it's not," Pearl said. "That's a currant out of one of the scones."

"I'm fairly sure it's a rat dropping," the man insisted.

Pearl bent down, picked it up, and put it in her mouth.

"See. It's a currant."

The man shook his head. "Oh? Maybe I was mistaken. Sorry. We'll carry on looking."

Amber, Pearl and me walked through to the front of the shop.

"You were lucky it was only a currant," I said.

Pearl rushed over to the sink, grabbed a glass of water and drank it as fast as she could. "That was no currant!"

Yuk! Gross!

We found a table near the window, and waited nervously until the inspectors had finished. Eventually, they re-joined us. The woman was very mouse-like and said almost nothing.

"I don't see any evidence of rat infestation," the man said. "But we did receive a report, so we have to take this very seriously."

"We were sabotaged," Amber said. "Someone planted them. We've never had rats!"

"Be that as it may, we have to check every report we receive. For now, I'm satisfied that there's no immediate hygiene issue. So I'm prepared to give you a warning on this occasion."

"A warning? What for?" Pearl was outraged. "They weren't our rats."

"Quiet, Pearl!" Amber tried to calm her sister.

"Here you are." He handed a sheet of paper to Pearl. "Read this very carefully and make sure you understand it. And, please be aware that if we receive any further reports, we may be forced to close the premises for a few days, or even longer. Do you understand?"

The twins nodded.

After the inspectors had left, Pearl thumped the table. "I'm going to kill Miles Best."

"Not if I get to him first." Amber fumed. "He's going to suffer for this."

"You can't just storm into Best Cakes, all guns blazing," I said. "You have to come up with a plan first."

"You're right." Amber took a deep breath. "We need to think of something really awful to do to those two."

I was still waiting for Daze and Mad, but it was Blaze who walked through the door first.

"Hi, Blaze. I didn't think I'd see *you* today."

"I wanted to catch you ahead of your meeting with Daze, to say that I've been giving a lot of thought to the offer from the other Rogue Retriever. It hasn't been an easy decision. Taze is really well regarded, and the prospect of being able to wear whatever colour catsuit I want, is very tempting. But in the end, I decided my loyalties lie with Daze. So I've thanked Taze for the opportunity, but said I won't be taking her up on her offer."

"I think you've made the right decision."

"Yeah, I think so too. Time will tell. But I just wanted to make sure that you don't mention any of this to Daze."

"No, of course I won't."

"Thanks. I wouldn't want to wreck my relationship with her for something that's not going to happen anyway."

"Don't worry. I won't say a word."

"Thanks, Jill. I'd better get off before Daze arrives."

Blaze had no sooner left than Daze and Mad arrived together.

"Before we do this," I said. "Are you sure we shouldn't tell Grandma and the other level six witches?"

"Definitely not." Daze insisted. "This is our one chance and we can't blow it. I've arranged for another three Rogue Retrievers to meet us in Washbridge."

"And I've got three other Ghost Hunters coming too," Mad said. "Between us, we should be more than a match for TDO and Destro. When they're in custody, then we can tell your grandmother and the others."

"We'd better not blow this." I was still worried. "Because if we do—"

"Don't even go there," Daze said. "Madeline and I have been discussing this, and we think you should stay here."

"Are you kidding? I was the one who found out when and where the meeting is going to be held."

"Yes, I know, but it's going to be very dangerous."

"I don't care! TDO has made my life a misery. If anyone should be in on this, it should be me."

"But—"

"No buts. I'm coming with you."

We made our way to the Fleur Hotel in Washbridge. The meeting was taking place on the seventh floor, and we had fifteen minutes before the scheduled start time. After we'd met up with the other Rogue Retrievers and Ghost Hunters, we split up into two groups. One group took the lift; my group took the stairs. At a prearranged time, we were going to storm the room, and hopefully capture the two most notorious villains in Candlefield and Ghost Town.

My heart was racing, and I could feel my hands shaking a little, so I held them at my side, and hoped no one would notice. Both groups made it to the conference room without any problems.

I could hear voices inside. This was it.

Daze counted down on her fingers. Three, two, one.

Daze and her fellow Rogue Retrievers kicked open the door, and we all stormed inside. Around the table there were five seats, but only three of them were occupied. Facing us, looking cool, calm and collected, were Ma Chivers, Alicia and Cyril. There was no sign of TDO or Destro.

"Morning, ladies," Ma Chivers said, as cool as you like. "Looking for someone?"

"Where are they?" I shouted.

"Where are who?"

"You know who. Where's TDO? Where's Destro?"

"I've no idea what you're talking about," Ma Chivers said, a smile playing across her lips. "I thought you'd come for your first lesson. You did say you wanted to study with me, didn't you? Surely you weren't lying?"

I wanted to jump over the table and rip her head off.

Except, of course, that I was no match for her, and she knew it.

"What went wrong?" Daze said.

"They must have known we were onto them. We've been set up. It's my fault, I should have realised it was all too easy."

"Don't worry about it, Jill. We'll get them sooner or later."

Daze, Mad and the others started towards the lift.

"You go ahead," I shouted after them. "I'll take the stairs."

After that crushing disappointment, I needed some time alone. I was furious that I'd been taken in so easily. Ma Chivers had played me for a fool.

When I reached the lobby, I bumped into a tall man with dark hair.

"Sorry." I tried to walk around him.

"It's Jill, isn't it?"

"Err—yeah? Who are you?"

"I'm your father."

Unlike with my birth mother, I'd never had a mental image of what my birth father might look like. But if I had tried to picture him, he would not have been anything like the man who now stood in front of me. This man was tall; at least six-three, had jet black hair, and was strikingly handsome for a man of his age.

"Jill, are you okay?"

I'd completely zoned out.

"I know you said you didn't want to see me, but it's important that we talk."

"I have nothing to say to you. I told Aunt Lucy to tell you that I didn't want to see you, and that you should stay away from me."

"I know, but it isn't that easy."

"You seem to have managed it for the first twenty-five years of my life. Why don't you keep doing what you've been doing?"

"Do you really think it was easy for me to stay away?"

"Apparently, it was. Why do you need to see me now? And why here, in this hotel? Why not in Candlefield?"

"I couldn't approach you in Candlefield. I knew that Lucy and Mirabel would be around, and let's face it they're not big fans of mine."

"Why would they be? What have you ever done to deserve their respect?"

"I don't expect you to understand, but I do need you to listen. There are things that we absolutely must discuss."

"Not now—not here. I'm not having a good day."

"When then? We have to speak soon. It's essential."

"I don't know."

He took a business card out of his pocket.

"My number is on here. Please give me a call, Jill. We have to talk. Your life may depend on it."

I took the card, and pushed it into my pocket. Anything to get rid of him.

"Okay. I'm going now." I side-stepped him.

"Please call me soon, Jill."

I set off apace, and after a few yards checked behind me. He was nowhere to be seen.

There were so many questions running around my head. Would I call him? What did he need to talk to me about that was so important? And why had he turned up here now? Had he really been looking for me today or was there some other reason why he was at the hotel?

***

On my way home, I checked in at the office to feed Winky. I'd no sooner put out his food than the colonel appeared.

"You made me jump."

"Sorry, Jill. I'm still not used to this ghost business yet. I haven't quite got the timing sorted out. I hope you don't mind me calling in for a chat. I haven't made many acquaintances yet in Ghost Town, so it's nice to see a familiar face."

"I'm glad you're here. I actually wanted a word with you."

"Really? What about?"

"My mother dropped in on me the other day."

"Darlene? Wonderful woman. I've only met her a couple of times, but she seems a good sort. What's the name of her husband again—Alberto?"

"That's right, yes."

"Welsh I believe?"

"Yes, surprisingly. Anyway, when she called by, she had another woman with her: Priscilla. Do you know her?"

"The name doesn't ring a bell."

"Well apparently, she has the hots for you, colonel."

"For me? Really?" He grinned.

"Yes. It seems she's rather smitten."

"I don't know what to say. It's been so long since I've

done any courting that I've almost forgotten how one goes about it. Did she say that she'd like to go on a date?"

"That was the impression I got, yes. My mother asked if I would mention it to you to see if you were open to the idea."

"Absolutely. Please tell her I'd be delighted to take her out for a meal or anything else she'd like to do."

"Okay. I'll ask my mother to let Priscilla know. I'm sure one of them will be in touch, and you can sort something out."

"That's wonderful. I'm really pleased I dropped in to see you, Jill. You've made my day."

If only my own love life was so simple.

Chapter 19

It was the day of the Levels AGM, and I'd arranged to meet Grandma at Aunt Lucy's. Aunt Lucy and Lester were on the sofa, smiling and chatting happily.

"Sorry to disturb you two, but I've arranged to meet Grandma here."

"It's okay, Jill. Lester has come up with a great idea for our honeymoon. He's suggested a cruise."

"That's a brilliant idea," I said. "Anywhere in particular?"

"That's what we're trying to decide now. There are two or three options we're considering."

When Aunt Lucy popped into the kitchen, Lester said in a low voice, "Thanks, Jill. You're a life saver."

"Are you ready or what?" Grandma came storming in.

"What are you talking about? I've been here for ten minutes." Sheesh.

"Are you sure you want Jill to go with you?" Aunt Lucy said.

"Why shouldn't she?"

"No reason. I just thought I should check you wouldn't rather I went."

"No. Jill will be fine." Grandma turned to me. "Get those folders, would you?"

"What? All of them?"

"Yes."

There was a stack of at least a dozen folders on the table.

"Do you have a bag I could put them in?"

"Can't you just carry them, girl?"

Whatever happened to the all-new, smiling Grandma? That hadn't lasted for very long.

"Just a minute, Jill. I'll get you a bag." Aunt Lucy opened a cupboard and brought out a couple of strong carrier bags.

"This lot weighs a ton," I said.

"Oh, stop moaning, woman." Grandma huffed. "Come on, let's get going or we'll be late."

"See you later, Jill." Aunt Lucy shot me a sympathetic look.

The AGM was being held in one of the rooms in the Town Hall. The last time I'd been there was on the day of Grandma's unsuccessful election campaign. I just hoped it didn't remind her or she'd be on my case about that again.

"Hurry up, Jill. We haven't got all day."

Once at the Town Hall, Grandma went charging up the steps. I was struggling to keep up with her. As soon as we entered the room where the meeting was to be held, all eyes seemed to be on me.

The room had been laid out with row after row of tables; each had two chairs behind it. At one end of the room was a huge stage with a banner draped across the front, which read: *Levels AGM*. A podium had been placed centre stage.

Grandma steered us towards the front of the room. As we squeezed past those witches who were already seated, a few of them huffed and puffed. I could hear them muttering under their breath, saying things like: *'What's she doing here? She's only a level three, isn't she?'*, and *'It's a disgrace. What does Mirabel think she's doing?'*.

If Grandma had heard them, she didn't comment. In

fact, she didn't react at all. When we eventually reached our seats, I put the folders on the table in front of Grandma.

"What's going on?" I whispered.

"What do you mean?"

"Everyone's staring at me."

"Does that matter?"

"I'd like to know why."

"They're not used to seeing a level three witch at the level six AGM."

"Maybe I shouldn't be here. Are you sure it's all right?"

"Of course it is. I wouldn't have brought you otherwise. There are no rules which dictate who my assistant can and can't be. It's just that assistants are usually level five witches. Anyway, you're here now, so they can like it or lump it."

I sat there, feeling very self-conscious as Grandma flicked through the papers on her desk. She was obviously psyching herself up for the speech she intended to give. Suddenly, someone thumped on our table. Both Grandma and me almost jumped out of our seats. It was Ma Chivers.

"What do you want, Chivers?" Grandma said.

"What's *she* doing here?" Ma Chivers fixed me with her gaze. I wanted the ground to open up and swallow me.

"She's my assistant. What's it to you?"

"She's not even level four. She doesn't belong here."

"I can have whoever I please as my assistant. If you'd bothered to check the rules of the AGM, you would know that."

"No one ever brings an assistant lower than a level five, Mirabel, *you* know that."

"There's a first time for everything, Chivers. Now, was there anything else you wanted?"

"Yes, I want her out of here. She's lowering the tone of the AGM."

"Listen to me, Chivers." Grandma pushed back her chair, and stood up. The two women were now wart to wart. "We're here today to vote on creating a new level, and I expect the motion to be passed. If it does, I guarantee you that Jill will be one of the first to attain level seven."

For a moment, I thought the two of them were going to scrap it out, but eventually Ma Chivers backed down. She shook her head in one last show of disgust, and then walked back to her own table.

"Did you really mean that, Grandma?"

"Mean what?"

"That I'll be a level seven witch one day."

"I only said that for effect. Don't let it go to your head. Level seven indeed!"

"But you said —"

"Hush! Can't you see I'm trying to prepare for my speech?"

There were five speakers against the motion to create a new level, and only two speakers in favour. The second of those was Grandma. When she took the stage, a silence fell over the room. She clearly commanded great respect amongst the witch community.

"Level six witches, you all know where I stand on this motion. For too long now, level six has been eroded. It seems that anyone with even a modicum of magical ability is promoted to the top level. When I became a level six witch, many, many centuries ago, it actually meant something. It was an elite level that many desired, but only few attained."

After she'd finished her speech, there was some polite applause, but I could see that a lot of witches were not clapping. Moments later, the vote was taken by a show of hands. I glanced around, and quickly realised that the motion had been defeated.

The chairman formally announced the outcome of the vote, "The motion to create a new level of witch—level seven—has been defeated."

"I should have known." Grandma thumped the table in anger. "We're never going to get these turkeys to vote for Christmas."

The rest of the AGM was fairly routine. A few more motions, a few more votes, but nothing very contentious. Grandma spoke very little during the rest of the time we were there.

As we made our way back to Aunt Lucy's, I thought I should say something.

"You made a very good speech."

"What?"

"Your speech, I thought it was very good. Very passionate."

"Didn't do much good though, did it? I should have known better than to expect that lot to see sense. They're too concerned with holding on to their *elite* status. Elite, my backside! It's not over yet. I shall raise this again at the next AGM, and at the one after that, and at as many as it takes until they see sense. Hopefully, by the time they do, you *will* be ready to join the *new elite*, but you'll have to put a lot more time and practice into your magic than you do at the moment."

"I put in a lot of practice."

"Not nearly enough. You have the ability to go all the way, Jill, but it won't just happen. It won't fall into your lap. If you want to be the very best, you'll have to work hard. Harder than all those others there today. You have to put in the hours. Do you understand?"

"Yes, Grandma."

***

I was absolutely shattered, but I couldn't get to sleep because of the noise. It sounded like voices. Was Betty practising her singing again? I checked my watch. It was just after eleven, and I was desperate for some sleep. If I didn't get some shut-eye, I'd be no good to anyone in the morning. I had to find the noise, and try to shut it down.

I threw on some clothes, made my way out of the flat, and stood in the corridor as I tried to work out where the noise was coming from. I soon tracked it down; it appeared to be coming from Mr Ivers' flat. If it had been anyone else, I would have thought there was a party going on inside, but Mr Ivers wasn't exactly a party animal. I doubted he had enough friends to have a party.

Once I was directly outside his door, I realised what it was. He was obviously watching a movie or something on TV. It was incredibly loud; the door was almost vibrating from the sound. What did he think he was playing at?

I knocked on the door, but there was no reply. I knocked again. There was still no reply. So I banged on the door as hard as I could, but still nothing. It wasn't really surprising. The volume was so loud that he probably couldn't hear himself think.

Then I had a brainwave. If I could sneak through his letterbox, maybe I could do something about the noise. I shrank myself, and then levitated until I was level with the letterbox. What an idiot! I was so small that I wasn't strong enough to lift the metal flap. A third spell was called for. Once I'd cast the 'power' spell, I was able to lift it easily.

Look at me—combining three spells. Level seven, here I come!

Once inside, I reversed the 'shrink' spell and made myself invisible. My poor eardrums were absolutely pounding, and once I was inside his living room, I could see why. He had installed a brand new home cinema system; the screen took up almost one whole wall. On either side of it were two humongous speakers which seemed to be vibrating. And there, on the sofa, sat Mr Ivers. How did his head not explode?

The remote control was on a small table next to the sofa. I pressed the button to turn down the volume. Mr Ivers looked confused, but then reached for the control, and turned it back up again. What was wrong with the man? No one needed the volume as loud as that. I turned it down again. Moments later, he turned it back up. I was getting nowhere fast, so this time I switched the screen off. Now he looked really confused, but switched it back on. I switched it off. He switched it on. Off. On. Off. On. Off.

Eventually, he yelled at the blank screen, "Stupid thing!"

And with that, he gave up and left the room. I waited a while, and when he didn't come back, I assumed he'd gone to bed.

Thank goodness. Now back home and bed for me too.

Chapter 20

I was shocked to receive a text message from Grandma. She hardly ever used a phone, and I'd never received a text message from her before. She wanted me to meet her at her house. What was that all about? I'd only been there once before when I'd been looking for her because the Everlasting Wool had stopped working. On that occasion, I'd found her close to despair; angry and upset with herself because her magic had failed her—if only temporarily. Grandma had no idea I'd been there that day, and if it was up to me, she would never find out.

I magicked myself over to Candlefield, and knocked on Grandma's front door. She shouted that I should come in. I found her in the living room, sitting next to a man I hadn't seen before. He was tall with striking red hair and a red beard. On the coffee table in front of them was a cage with two budgerigars in it. I had no idea that Grandma kept budgies; she'd certainly never mentioned it. Maybe they belonged to the man.

"Thanks for coming over, Jill," Grandma said. "I wanted you to meet Horace."

"Pleased to meet you, Horace." I offered my hand.

His grip was strong—very strong for a man of his age. His hand was extremely cold.

"I've heard a lot about you from Mirabel; I feel like I already know you."

Horace was not at all what I'd been expecting. For some reason, I'd assumed he would be a meek character—someone who would kowtow to Grandma as most people did. But incredibly, he seemed to be the dominant personality of the two. Grandma kept glancing at him—as if seeking approval. This was something I'd never seen before. Grandma always took the lead, and liked to have her say, but today, she seemed to defer to Horace.

"I hope to get to know all of Mirabel's family much better in the coming months," he said.

The more he spoke, the more he gave me the creeps, but I had no idea why. And yet, Grandma seemed perfectly comfortable, if a little subdued, in his presence. What was it about him? I couldn't quite put my finger on it.

"It's very nice to have met you, Horace." If a little creepy. "But I do need to get back. There are some things I have to attend to."

"Before you go, Jill, there is one other thing," Grandma said. "I don't think you've met my budgies."

"I didn't know you kept them."

"The yellow one is called Amber, and the green one, that's Pearl."

I smiled at the joke, but then I saw *it* in her face. She wasn't joking.

"Grandma—you didn't. You haven't. Please tell me these aren't the twins."

"Those girls never learn." She cackled. "I thought the donkeys' ears might have taught them a lesson, but no. As if they could spy on me, and get away with it."

"Grandma, you can't do this. You have to turn them back now."

"Don't get in such a flap, Jill. The spell will only last for another hour. Here."

She picked up the cage and handed it to me.

"Take them back to Cuppy C, will you? And be sure to let them out of the cage before the hour is up otherwise it'll get awfully cramped in there." She cackled again.

I couldn't get out of the house fast enough. When I glanced down at the cage, both budgies were tweeting at me. I could sense the twins begging me to help them. Once at Cuppy C, I hurried upstairs to Amber's bedroom. When I opened the door of the cage, the two budgies flew out. They fluttered desperately around the room, and kept trying to land on my shoulder. I hate birds flying around me, so I left the room and closed the door behind me.

Just under an hour later, I heard footsteps coming down the stairs.

"I did warn you," I said. "I told you not to mess with Grandma."

"I know." Amber sighed. "We're idiots."

"We'll never do it again." Pearl brushed a feather from her hair. "That's for sure."

"So anyway, how was life as a budgie?" I laughed. "I bet it was really *tweet*."

"Shut up, Jill."

***

I'd decided to give the Neighbourhood Watch a try. After all, if Kathy and Peter could do it, why couldn't I? The leaflet had said the meetings were held on Thursday nights.

When I arrived at the community hall, there were several cars in the car park. The woman standing just inside the door was a witch.

"Hi," I said. "Am I in the right place for the Neighbourhood Watch meeting?"

She looked puzzled for a moment. "Do you mean Z-Watch?"

"Yeah."

"Then you're in the right place."

"Who's in charge?"

"Ike Cann."

"I can?"

"Not 'I can'. Ike Cann. That's him over there." She pointed to a very tall, broad man with greying hair, who I immediately recognised as being a werewolf. When I glanced around at the other people who were waiting for proceedings to start, it quickly became apparent that they were all sups. That couldn't possibly be a coincidence.

Ike Cann walked to the front of the hall. "If you would all just take a seat now, please, we'll get the meeting underway." He caught my eye. "First time?"

I nodded.

"Pleased you could join us. I'm Ike."

"Jill. Jill Gooder."

"Oh yes. I read about you in The Candle. Take a seat, Jill."

I sat next to a male vampire who flashed me a rather scary smile.

"Could I ask a question?" I put up my hand.

"Of course," Ike said. "Fire away."

"Why aren't there any humans in this Neighbourhood Watch? After all, they make up the majority of the population around here."

A few people laughed, and I felt as though I was missing the joke. Ike hushed everyone.

"Z-Watch is not a Neighbourhood Watch as such, Jill."

"Oh? I assumed it was the Neighbourhood Watch for the Zander estate?"

"Z-Watch is actually short for Zombie Watch."

Huh? "Zombie Watch?"

"That's right."

"I don't understand."

"Let me give you some background. As I understand it, you've lived among humans all of your life?"

I nodded.

"In that case you probably won't know the history of the zombies."

"I didn't think there were such things."

"Yes, but then until quite recently, you probably didn't think there were witches, wizards, vampires or werewolves either?"

That was true. "So, there *are* zombies?"

"A few, yes. Zombies are neither sup nor human. They're—well—undead. And to be honest, they're a bit of a nuisance."

Everyone in the room nodded.

"The thing is," he continued. "They love to draw attention to themselves: walking around, flailing their arms about, and eating people's brains. It's not the sort of thing that goes unnoticed."

"I guess not."

"If they're allowed to roam free or more accurately, hobble free." He laughed at his own joke. "It's going to be noticed by the humans, and that's bad for us all. Once the humans realise they're living alongside zombies, they might also realise that there are sups in their neighbourhood too. So it's in all of our interests to stop the zombies drawing attention to themselves. Hence, Z-Watch."

"And how exactly does Z-Watch work?"

"We have branches throughout the human world. It's

our job to keep an eye open for zombies. If and when any of them rise from the dead, we make sure we dispatch them pretty quickly. Before a human spots them."

"Dispatch them? You mean kill them?"

He laughed. "We can hardly kill them, Jill. They're not alive. But then, they're not dead either. We eliminate them."

"How do you do that?"

"The method varies from sup to sup. For a witch such as yourself, the best method is to use the 'thunderbolt' spell. You're familiar with that, I assume?"

I nodded.

"If you aim the thunderbolt at the centre of the zombie's forehead that will blow the thing to smithereens. No more zombie."

"I see."

"So, now you know what we do, I'm hoping you'll agree to join our ranks."

"How much time will it require because I'm rather busy most days."

"Most of the people here have full time jobs. We just ask you to keep a lookout, and if you see a zombie then press the Z-Call button."

"What's that?"

He took something out of his pocket, and handed it to me. It was a small silver box with a single button on the front.

"What does this do?"

"If you spot a zombie, press the button, and that will alert all the other Z-Watch members in the vicinity."

"Can I keep this?"

"Yes. Make sure you have it with you at all times. If you

spot a zombie, press the button or if you feel the little button vibrate, that means another member has spotted a zombie. When that happens, call the number printed on the back, and you'll be given details of where the zombie has been spotted."

"Does that happen very often? Are there many zombies?"

"Not many. Probably only five or six in this area a year, on average. Most of the time you needn't worry about it. It's just a question of being on call. We'll also need you to choose a passphrase."

"What's that for?"

"Zombies may be undead, but they can be quite cunning. It has been known for a zombie to kill a Z-Watch member, then take the button, and use it to call other members to him. Those who respond are caught unawares and fall victim themselves. To avoid this situation, we will always ask you to quote your passphrase. Do you have a phrase in mind?"

"How about 'crazy just got crazier'?"

"Sure. That's fine. 'Crazy just got crazier' it is."

***

When I got back to my flat, I bumped into Mr Ivers.

"Hello, Jill. How are you?"

"Okay, except that I haven't been sleeping very well."

"Oh, dear. Why's that?"

"The noise from your home cinema has been keeping me awake."

"How did you know I'd bought one?"

"Because I can hear the stupid thing from my flat."

"I'm sorry if I've kept you awake. I didn't realise it was as loud as that."

"So will you keep it down?"

"You don't have to worry. I've sent it back. The stupid volume kept lowering itself. And then the screen would switch itself on and off. I've decided to abandon the idea of home cinema; I'd rather go to the multiplex, anyway. I don't suppose you'd like to come with me next week, would you?"

"Thanks, but I'll have to take a rain check." The next time it rains for forty days and forty nights, give me a call.

Chapter 21

When I walked into the office, Mrs V scrambled to push something into her drawer. This was becoming something of a habit. What was she trying to hide? Curiosity had now got the better of me.

"Morning, Jill." She gave me an innocent look, but I knew better.

"Morning, Mrs V. Is it my imagination, or do you hide something every time I walk into the office?"

She blushed, and I knew that I'd got her.

"I don't know what you mean, dear."

"Come on, Mrs V. I know something's going on. Every time I walk in, you push something into that top drawer of yours."

"I think you must be mistaken."

"Okay then. So, if I open that drawer—"

"No, you mustn't do that." She put her hand on it to hold it shut.

"So, you *are* hiding something. I hope you haven't been looking at naughty magazines."

"Don't be ridiculous. How could you even think such a thing?"

"What am I meant to think? You're obviously hiding something."

"All right." She sighed. "If you must know."

She opened the drawer, and pulled out what at first glance looked like a pile of knitting.

"Is that it?" I was rather disappointed. I'd been expecting something scandalous.

"It's bad enough, isn't it?"

"Knitting? Why all the secrecy?"

"Don't you know anything, Jill? Look." She pointed at the needle.

"That's a strange looking knitting needle."

"That's because it's a crochet hook. I've been crocheting."

I laughed. "Hold on a minute. Are you trying to tell me that all the subterfuge was because you've been crocheting?"

"Of course."

"Why? What does it matter?"

"*What does it matter*? I've gone over to the dark side. If my yarnies were to ever find out, they'd cast me out of the inner circle. I'd be a pariah."

"Are you serious? Can't people knit *and* crochet?"

"Amateurs, probably, yes. But when you're at my level, it's a matter of pride. Knitters look down on the crocheters, and vice versa."

"So, why are you doing it?"

"I couldn't help myself, dear. I've had this crochet hook for years. I can't remember when or even why I bought it. Anyway, the other day, I was having a clear out, and I spotted it. I thought, 'Shall I? Shan't I?' Then something evil must have taken hold of me because the next thing I knew, I was crocheting. And what's worse, I actually enjoyed it. I wish I'd never found the stupid thing."

"You don't need to hide it from me."

"I thought you might mention it to your grandmother."

"I would never do that."

"Thanks. Even so, I'd better keep it under wraps because if it was ever to get out, things could be very difficult for me."

"Does this mean that you've given up on the knitting?"

"Of course not. Knitting will always be my first love. I've got several projects on the go at the moment. But every now and then, I find I need a quick crochet fix."

"Well, I say go for it. And you don't have to hide it from me. My lips are sealed."

"Thanks, Jill. You're a good friend."

I went through to my office, and took a deep breath. Who knew there were such rivalries in the world of yarn?

"What's up with the old bag lady this morning?" Winky yawned.

"She has a few things on her mind."

"Is it because she's been crocheting?"

"How did you know?"

"I make it my business to know everything that happens in this office."

"You mustn't tell anyone."

"Really? Oh dear, because I was just about to put a post on FelineSocial."

"Winky, you can't do that. Mrs V will be furious with me. She'll think I've let it out of the bag."

"I suppose I could be persuaded to keep it quiet."

"Salmon?"

"Hmm—that would do nicely. Red, not pink, obviously."

***

That evening, back at my flat, there was a knock at the door. I opened it to find Ike Cann.

"Hi, Ike. What brings you here?"

"Before I can answer, I'll need you to say the

passphrase."

"Sorry?"

"The passphrase. I just need you to say it."

"Isn't the passphrase meant to be used when someone makes a phone call, so you know that it's them?"

"That's right."

"But, you're here. You can see it's me."

"I can see someone who looks like you. I need to be one hundred per cent sure."

"Of course. The passphrase? What was it again?"

"If I told you, that would rather defeat the object, wouldn't it?"

"I suppose so. Was it custard creams rule?"

"No. That wasn't it."

"Blueberry muffins are the best?"

"No, that wasn't it either."

"Oh, yeah. I remember. Crazy just got crazier."

"That's it! Thanks, Jill. I just had to be sure. Can I come in?"

"Of course. What can I do for you?"

"I wanted to come and see you in person because we've had an orange alert."

"I don't think my button buzzed."

"It's only a preliminary warning at the moment. No one's actually spotted a zombie, but one or two people have picked up the vibe."

"The vibe?"

"Some of our senior werewolf members get a sense of when there's going to be a zombie incident. I don't know why, but from what I understand, their ears start to itch."

"And that's happened?"

"Yeah. A couple of them have reported an ear-itch

situation."

"So what exactly do I need to do?"

"Nothing yet. But because you're new to this, I thought I'd come over in person to give you a heads-up. The orange level warning is in the West Breighton area."

"West Breighton?"

"Do you know it?"

"That's where my sister lives."

"In that case, it might be an idea to get over there. Just in case."

***

I was beginning to regret having signed up for Z-Watch. I'd been blissfully oblivious to the fact that there were zombies around. Now, I had to be on constant alert for them. After what Ike had just told me, I wanted to check the neighbourhood around Kathy's house. I couldn't have the undead attacking my nephew or niece. They could have Kathy, though.

What? It was a joke. Sheesh!

I couldn't let Kathy, Peter or the kids see me because they'd probably invite me into the house, and I really needed to be outside if I was going to keep watch for zombies. I parked a few streets away, and took refuge in the bus shelter at the end of their road. The shelter had glass on the front and back, but the sides were made of concrete. That worked out well because it meant I couldn't be seen from Kathy's house.

An elderly woman sat next to me in the bus shelter. She didn't speak; she was too busy knitting. And if I wasn't mistaken, she was using Everlasting Wool. A few moments later, a bus pulled up. It was the only bus that travelled that particular route, so naturally the bus driver expected me to board.

"I'm not actually waiting for a bus."

He gave me a puzzled look, but went on his way.

I still couldn't convince myself there were actually zombies around. I mean, surely if there were, I would've seen one before now? Or at the very least, I would have heard something about them. It's the sort of story that The Bugle would delight in. Still, I had to be vigilant. If there *were* any zombies, I needed to spot them quickly before any humans did. We didn't want mass panic.

I'd been there for about fifteen minutes when suddenly a car pulled up in front of me. It was Peter, Kathy, and the kids. They must have been out somewhere, and were headed home.

"Jill?" Peter said, sticking his head out of the window. "What are you doing there?"

"Waiting for a bus."

"Where's your car?"

"It broke down a couple of streets away, so I was going to get the bus back into town."

"Why didn't you go to our house?"

"I did, but you weren't in."

"Well, we're back now. Jump in. You can have a cup of tea, and then I'll take you home. You can call the breakdown service from there."

"It's okay. I'll take the bus."

"Don't be silly. Get in."

"Come on, Auntie Jill," Lizzie shouted.

"Yeah, come on, Auntie Jill." Mikey hit his drum.

I squeezed into the back seat with the kids.

Kathy looked back at me. "Are you sure your car has broken down?"

"Of course it did. Why else would I be taking the bus?"

"I don't know. Something doesn't seem right."

"You know your trouble, Kathy? You're way too suspicious."

"I wonder why."

Once we were inside the house, Kathy sent Peter into the kitchen to make us all a cup of tea. She had no custard creams as usual, so I settled for a cupcake. Very nice it was, too. But I was conscious that I shouldn't be sitting inside, enjoying tea and cake. I should be outside, zombie watching.

I went over to the front window, and looked up and down the street. I couldn't see any undead. Then, I walked through to the kitchen, and checked the rear of the house. Still nothing.

"Jill!" Kathy shouted.

"Yeah?"

"What are you doing?"

"Just looking at the garden."

"It's dark. You can't even see the garden. Why don't you come and sit down? You're making me dizzy."

"I will in a moment."

"What are you looking for?"

"Nothing. I've just got cramp; I need to stretch my legs."

Just then, I felt a vibration in my pocket. For a moment, I thought it was my phone, but then realised it was the Z-Call button. I had to phone in to Z-Watch.

"I feel a bit woozy," I said. "I'm just going to step

outside for a moment to get some fresh air."

"Are you okay? What are you up—?"

I didn't give Kathy a chance to finish; I was already out of the back door.

It was Ike who answered the call. "Ike, it's Jill."

"What's the passphrase?"

"Are we going to do this, *every* time? Crazy just got crazier."

"Okay. Look, Jill, we have reliable information that there's a zombie on the prowl. It's been seen on Mill Street. Do you know it?"

"That's where I am now."

"In that case, it can't be far away from you. Do you know what to do if you see it?"

"Sure."

"Okay, be careful. I'll get some other people over there as soon as I can."

"Right."

I made my way to the front of the house, and looked up and down the street. There was no sign of the zombie, so I began to walk slowly down the road. When I reached the far end, I heard something. A kind of shuffling sound. It seemed to come from the back of the house immediately to my right. I ran into the back yard, and there it was. A more horrible creature you could not wish to see. It was a man or at least what was left of him. One of his arms was barely attached to his body; one of his legs was twisted around on itself. He was shuffling along just like the zombies in every bad X-rated movie I'd ever seen.

He sniffed the air, and then turned to face me. The next moment, he began to shuffle my way. He was hungry, and my brains were on the menu. Ike had said I should use a thunderbolt, and that I had to hit him in the forehead. I'd always thought zombies couldn't move very fast, but he seemed to be getting closer much too quickly for my liking. I fired a thunderbolt and missed. He was only a few feet away now. I didn't want to be a zombie's dinner! I fired again. This time, I hit him square in the centre of the forehead, and he disintegrated into a cloud of smoke.

Phew! That was close.

I rang Ike again.

"What's the passphrase?"

"Ike! I only spoke to you two minutes ago."

"Passphrase, please."

"Crazy just got crazier."

"Right. How's it going?"

"I found it, and destroyed it."

"Good work. Well done."

"I've got to go, Ike. I'll catch up with you later."

I hurried back to Kathy's.

"Where've you been, Jill? I checked all around the house, and couldn't see you anywhere."

"I was just getting some fresh air. I felt a little queasy."

"No kidding. You look like death warmed up."

Chapter 22

I'd no sooner walked into the office than Mad came charging in. She was dressed in her librarian clothes, and had obviously been running.

"What's wrong, Mad?"

"Are you all right, young lady?" Mrs V looked very concerned.

"Yeah. I'm okay, thanks."

"Are you sure?" I said. "You don't look it."

"Would you like me to get you a glass of water?" Mrs V offered.

"No, honestly, I'm fine."

"You'd better come through to my office." I led the way. "Are you being chased by a ghost or something?"

"Far worse than that. Do you mind if I sit down?"

"Help yourself. So who were you running from?"

"I was just on my way to the coffee shop when I saw my ex-boyfriend."

"I thought he was still living in London?"

"He's supposed to be. I've no idea what he's doing here. He must have contacted my mother; she's just stupid enough to have told him that I was back here. She hasn't got the brains she was born with."

"I thought he'd dumped you for your friend?"

"Thanks for the reminder, Jill."

"Sorry."

"Maybe my *former* best friend has dumped him already. Or he's realised what he's missing. Either way, I don't want to see him. And I certainly can't let him see me dressed like this."

"What do you mean?"

"It's not exactly how he's used to seeing me dress. I've no idea how I'd explain that I'm working as a librarian. Hopefully, my mother hasn't already told him."

At that point we both heard an almighty bang as the door of the outer office crashed open. I could hear Mrs V shouting at someone, and a man shouting right back at her.

"That's him," Mad said. "He must have followed me. What am I going to do?"

"It's okay. Don't panic."

In walked a tall, good-looking, if rather thuggish young man who had tattoos on both arms. He was wearing ripped jeans, and trainers which had seen better days.

"Mad?" He stared at her. "What's going on? Why are you dressed like that?"

"Hello, Troy."

Troy? Really?

"I asked you a question," he yelled. "Why are you dressed like that? And why is your hair in a bun?"

"More to the point, why are you here, Troy?"

"I came to get you, didn't I?"

"Well you've had a wasted journey. We're done."

"Don't be daft. Me and you were meant to be together."

"In that case, what were you doing with Cynthia?"

"That was nothing. We were just messing around."

"That's not what I'd call it."

"Yeah, but it didn't mean anything. I'd had a drink. You know what I'm like when I've had a drink."

"Stupid, you mean?"

"Can't we talk about this? You don't want to live up here; you always said you hated Washbridge."

"Not as much as I hate you—and Cynthia."

"I still don't know what you're doing dressed like that. You look like a librarian or something. Where are your normal clothes?"

"Just leave, Troy."

"I'm not going anywhere until you tell me what's going on."

This conversation was going nowhere fast. It was time for me to step in.

"Troy," I shouted.

"Huh?" He turned to look at me, and when he did, I cast the 'forget' spell.

"Quick, Mad." I grabbed her arm. "You shoot off before he comes around properly."

"Okay, Jill. Thanks."

"Where am I?" Troy said. "What's this place?"

"This is a private investigator's office. I'm Jill Gooder. Did you want me for something?"

"What do you mean?"

"You're in my office. I assume you wanted to see me?"

"No. I don't really know why I'm here."

"Well in that case, maybe you should leave."

"I remember. I was looking for Mad."

"Mad what?"

"Madeline. She's my girlfriend. I was looking for her. But then — I don't know what happened."

"I think you'd better leave now."

"Okay. Yeah. Sorry. Bye then."

And with that, Troy left.

***

Minutes later, Jack Maxwell turned up.

"Do you have a minute, Jill?"

"Sure. Would you like a coffee?"

"No, I can't stay. There's something I have to tell you, and I wanted to do it face to face."

"That sounds serious."

"I'm being transferred."

"Transferred where?"

"To the north of England."

"But you've only been in Washbridge for five minutes."

"I know. It doesn't usually happen this way. I'd assumed I'd be here for at least three years. Then, out of the blue, I got the message earlier today that there's a staff shortage in Westmonton. And, for some reason, my name came out of the hat."

"Can't you turn it down?"

"I did try. I said I'd barely scratched the surface here, and wanted time to make my mark, but it didn't cut any ice. As far as the force is concerned, orders are orders. If they say, 'jump,' I have to jump. If they say, 'Go to the north of England,' then that's where I have to go."

"When do you leave?"

"A couple of days, tops."

"I see."

I didn't know what to say. We hadn't been in a relationship as such, but I had begun to feel as though we were getting closer. And the fact that he wanted to deliver his news in person, suggested he might feel the same.

"I know you and I got off to a bad start," he said. "But since then, I think we've worked well together."

"Wow! Coming from you, that's quite the compliment."

He wasn't kidding about the bad start. When he'd first arrived in Washbridge, he'd been a real pain in the backside, and had made my life as difficult as he could.

Right from the start, he'd made it perfectly clear he didn't want me anywhere near any of his investigations. It was only later that I'd discovered the reason for his dislike of private investigators. He'd been involved in a kidnapping case in his previous post, which had gone badly wrong with the result that the hostage had been killed. The blame for that had fallen fairly and squarely with a negligent, private investigator.

"Anyway," he said. "I just thought I'd come around and let you know. I'll leave a note for my successor to tell him that he should cut you some slack. At least more than I did in the beginning."

"Thanks, Jack. I appreciate that."

"Not at all, you deserve it. You're no mug, and I know that if it hadn't been for your help, there would still be a number of unsolved cases on our books." He leaned forward and gave me a peck on the cheek, and then left.

I stared at the door until long after he had gone. I'd really blown it this time. He'd obviously felt closer to me than I'd realised, and yet I'd been so blind or so stubborn that I hadn't acted upon it. And now, it was too late.

I wiped away a tear.

"Jill?"

I nearly jumped out of my skin, and turned to find Grandma sitting on the sofa.

"How long have you been there?"

"Long enough to see the waterworks. What's wrong with you, woman?"

"Nothing, I've just got something in my eye."

"Really? I thought it was because that detective friend of yours was leaving."

"You heard all of that?"

"I hear everything. You should know that."

I wiped my eyes again. I didn't want to cry in front of Grandma. "He's just a friend."

"Hmm, that's not what it looked like to me."

"Why are you here, Grandma?"

"I came to check up on you."

"Why?"

"Because it's the Compass competition in a few days' time, and I wanted to make sure that you're getting in plenty of practice. A team is only as good as its weakest link."

"I'm practising, Grandma. I've been doing nothing else."

"Good. I don't want this *Jack* business to get in the way. Understand?"

"Understood, captain!"

"The Compass competition must be your top priority. Forget everything else, and just focus on your magic. I want you to be on tip-top form on the day. Got it?"

"Got it."

"Good."

***

I really didn't feel like going around to Kathy's, but I'd promised to go over for coffee. I should have been practising for the Compass competition, but that wasn't what was on my mind. It was the thought of Jack Maxwell's transfer. I never realised just how much he meant to me until he said he was leaving. I was such an idiot. If I'd allowed our relationship to develop instead of flitting back and forth between him, Drake, Luther and every other man who happened to wander into my path, then who knows what might have happened? But it was too late now. In a few days' time, he'd be gone, and that would be it.

"Jill?" Kathy made me jump. I'd zoned out while drinking my coffee. "What's wrong with you?"

"Nothing. Why?"

"Don't lie. I can tell something's wrong."

"It's nothing, honestly."

"You haven't touched your custard creams, so don't tell me nothing's wrong. You never turn your nose up at a custard cream."

"I'm not really hungry."

"What's happened? You might as well tell me because I'm not letting up until you do."

"If you must know, Jack Maxwell is leaving."

"For good?"

"Yeah. He's been transferred to the north of England somewhere."

"But he hasn't been here for very long, has he?"

"He said it was rare to be transferred again so quickly. He thought he'd be here for at least three years. But the order came through, and apparently there's nothing he can do about it."

"When did he tell you?"

"Earlier today. He came to the office."

"How has he taken it?"

"He wasn't happy."

"Because he's got to relocate? Or because he's leaving you?"

"A bit of both, I think. That's what makes it worse. I didn't even realise that he cared. Anyway, it doesn't matter now. He's leaving. It's my own fault; I should've listened to you."

"Whoa, steady on." Kathy looked shocked. "Now you really have got me worried. If you're actually admitting that you should've listened to me, something must be seriously wrong."

"It's true though, isn't it? You told me it was time to take my relationships seriously; to pick someone and stick with them. I should've listened to you. I liked Jack from the get-go even though he was a pain in the backside. There was just something about him. I've messed up big time."

"Don't be so hard on yourself. It's not like it's *all* your fault. He should have done something about it, too."

"It doesn't matter now. He's going, and that's all there is to it."

I was just about to leave Kathy's when my phone rang. It was Jack. When I showed her the caller ID, she nodded and went through to the kitchen to give me some privacy.

"Hi, Jill. I thought you'd want to know my news."

"I thought I already did?"

"Everything's changed."

"Changed how?"

"The transfer's been cancelled. I'm not leaving."

"You're not? How come?"

"Beats me. It was signed, sealed, and delivered as far as I knew. Yesterday, my boss said there was no chance of the transfer being reversed, but then an hour ago, I was called into his office. He said I'm staying put for at least three years."

"Did he say why?"

"I don't think he knows why. He said the order had

come from *high-up*—from a Commander Millbright. My boss had never heard of him."

I was gobsmacked. Commander Millbright? That could not be a coincidence.

"Jill, are you still there?"

"Sorry, yes. That's great news. I'm really pleased. Thanks for letting me know."

"I guess I'm going to have to put up with you for a while longer." He laughed.

"I guess so. I'll try not to give you too much grief."

"Look, we should go out for a drink, to celebrate."

"I'd like that."

"Okay. I'd better get going. Duty calls. I'll be in touch to arrange something."

"All right, Jack. See you later."

Kathy came back through. "That sounded like good news."

"His transfer's been cancelled. He's staying in Washbridge."

"That was a quick change of plan."

"I know. Apparently someone high up in the force vetoed the move."

"You must be thrilled."

"I am. Yes."

"I hope you've learned your lesson, and take advantage of this. Don't blow it a second time."

"I won't."

"I know you, Jill. You'll go back to how you were, just messing around."

"I won't. He's already said we should go out on a date to celebrate. Maybe that will be the start of something?"

"Make sure it is, because you don't want to find yourself in this same position in three-years' time when he does move on."

"I know. You're right."

As I walked to the car, I remembered what Jack had said. Commander Millbright? It must have been Grandma. She'd somehow managed to get Jack's transfer cancelled. But why? Maybe I'd misjudged her?

Chapter 23

The next morning, I was feeling as happy as a lark; all was well with the world for once. Nothing could spoil my good mood.

"Hello, Jill."

I'd spoken too soon. It was Dougal Andrews, or as I still thought of him, Dougal Bugle.

"What do you want, Dougal?"

"That's no way to greet a friend." He had his trademarked false smile plastered across his face.

"If you were a friend, I'd be civil. But seeing as you're an obnoxious scumbag, I don't feel the need."

"I know you don't really mean that."

"I'm on my way to work. I don't have time to talk to you."

"What did you think of the slavery article?"

"I thought it was absolute trash. But then, so is everything printed in that rag of yours."

"The Bugle is not a 'rag'. I'll have you know we've just recruited one of the country's top investigative reporters."

"If he's agreed to work on The Bugle, he can't be anything special."

"It's not a 'he', it's a 'she'. Susan Hall—you've probably heard of her. She's won all kinds of awards."

"Can't say I have, and I really don't care. Oh, and if I was you, I'd steer well clear of my P.A."

"Your slave, you mean?"

"Annabel Versailles is no one's slave. But I can tell you this for nothing. If she gets her hands on you, you'll wish you'd never been born."

Dougal laughed it off. But then he probably spent most

of his day being on the wrong end of threats. He was born to do that job; he was a slimeball if ever there was one.

"Get out of the way, Dougal. I've got work to do."

"Wouldn't you like to know what my next story is going to be?"

"Let me think about that for a moment. Err — no, I don't give a monkey's."

"I know you do really. There's a rumour going around of unethical practices in one of Washbridge's newest retailers."

"Dougal, you're confusing me with somebody who cares."

"As a member of the Washbridge community, you should care if one of the shops in the area is cheating people."

"Get lost, Dougal!"

"It's that new wool shop. You may have heard of it: Ever A Wool Moment, I think it's called."

My heart sank. What had Dougal dug up on 'Ever'? Whatever it was, it wouldn't be good. "I've seen the shop, yes."

"It seems they're making promises that are simply impossible to keep. Apparently, they're offering a product called Everlasting Wool. I ask you, how can wool last forever?"

"Maybe it's a new invention?"

"Don't be ridiculous. You know as well as I do that a ball of wool can't go on forever. And, that's not the only thing. They're selling One-Size Knitting Needles too. Apparently, instead of having to buy different needles for different projects, this new-fangled gadget is meant to resize itself magically."

"I'm not interested. Why are you telling me this?"

"Like I said, I figured that as a member of the Washbridge community, you'd want to be made aware. You'll be able to read the full story when it appears shortly. I'm going down there now to check a few facts."

"Good luck with that."

As Dougal went whistling on his merry way, I made a quick call to Kathy, who I knew would be at work by now.

"Kathy, do you remember that article The Bugle printed under my name?"

"The hatchet job on the police?"

"That's the one. Well, I just bumped into Dougal Andrews, the guy who wrote it. He's a real nasty piece of work. He did another article last week on Mrs V, which made out that I was treating her like a slave."

"Oh dear." Kathy laughed. "I missed that one."

"I wouldn't laugh just yet. He's just told me that he's investigating a new shop in town which is cheating the Washbridge customers. Apparently that shop is Ever A Wool Moment."

"What do you mean, 'cheating'?"

"He's suspicious of Everlasting Wool and One-Size Knitting Needles, and I think he's on his way over there right now."

"What am I supposed to do? I don't know any more about how they work than he does."

"I just thought I'd better warn you. If I was you, I'd tell Grandma he's on his way. He's a slippery character, but if anyone can handle him, Grandma probably can."

***

"That cat of yours is at it again," Mrs V said. "There's a lot of meowing coming from in there."

"Don't worry. I'll get it sorted."

When I opened the door to my office, I couldn't believe my eyes. There was a long line of cats snaking around the room. They were all queuing to go into a small tent which had been erected just in front of my desk. On the front of the tent was a sign which read:

'Your fortune told by Madam Winkesca. Ten pounds a time'.

Madam Winkesca? I'd give him Madam Winkesca.

I made my way straight to the front of the queue much to the annoyance of the other cats.

"Hey, what do you think you're doing?"

"There's a queue here."

"Hey, you! Get in line."

I ignored them, and crawled on hands and knees through the flap, and into the tent. Winky was dressed in a robe and veil. On the table in front of him was a crystal ball.

"What's going on, Winky?"

"That's Madam Winkesca to you."

"What are you up to?"

"What does it look like?"

"It looks like you're conning these cats out of ten pounds."

"How dare you! Madam Winkesca can see the future."

"Rubbish."

"Would you like me to prove it to you?"

"Go on then."

"It'll cost you ten pounds."

"Get lost."

"I'll do you a special deal. Seeing as it's you. Five pounds."

Curiosity (or stupidity) got the better of me, and I handed over the cash. Winky began to rub the crystal ball slowly.

"I see a man," he said. "His initials are J and N. No, wait a minute, make that J and M. He's a good friend of yours."

I sneered. Winky had seen Jack Maxwell in the office numerous times. "Is that all you've got?"

"He's going to receive bad news about his job."

"Well, that's where you're wrong. The bad news was cancelled. Jack Maxwell isn't being transferred. I've got a good mind to tell those cats out there that you're a fraud."

"That's your call. I just thought you could use the money."

"What money?"

"I was going to give you ten percent of my takings for the use of your office."

"Fifty percent."

"Twenty."

"Thirty."

"Done."

***

There was precious little point in trying to work in the office while Madam Winkesca was still in residence, so I decided to get a coffee at Coffee Triangle. I'd just stepped out onto the street when I bumped into Drake who looked very concerned about something.

"Hi, Jill. I was just on my way to see you."

"I needed to get out of the office for some fresh air. How are you settling into the flat?"

He frowned. "This probably sounds ridiculous and even a touch paranoid, but I can't shake the feeling that someone is spying on me whenever I'm in there."

"What do you mean, spying on you?" As if I didn't already know.

"It might sound a bit strange, but it's almost as though I can feel someone's eyes burning into me whenever I'm in the flat. I do realise how ridiculous that sounds."

Not all that ridiculous.

"Is it possible someone has you under surveillance?" I said. "Do you have any business rivals who might be after trade secrets or anything like that?"

"I wouldn't have thought so, but I guess it's always possible. Do you have any equipment which you can use to check for bugging devices and hidden cameras?"

"Not personally, but there are a couple of people I use for that kind of work."

"Do you think you could get someone to do a sweep of my flat to see if there's anything there?"

"Of course. If you let me have a key, I'll get someone over there."

"Thanks, Jill, that's great." He handed me a key. "I really do appreciate this. Anyway, I don't want to take up any more of your time. I'd better get going."

I didn't need to have the flat swept to know what the problem was. I'd experienced it first-hand on the one occasion when I'd visited Drake's flat. I'd seen Grandma's face looking out at me from the TV screen, and again from the mirror. I had no idea how she was doing it, but magic was obviously involved. I'd assumed she'd done it so she could keep an eye on me, so why would she be watching Drake when I wasn't there?

I'd have to have a few choice words with Grandma, and see what she had to say for herself.

***

"Is she in?" I asked Kathy who was behind the counter in Ever A Wool Moment.

"She's in the back."

"Has Dougal Andrews been to see her?"

"Yes, but he didn't stay long."

"Did Grandma seem upset?"

"No. She seemed ultra-friendly with him when he left."

That didn't make any sense. I'd expected her to be livid, and to exact some awful retribution on Dougal.

When I burst into the back office, Grandma was staring into space.

"I have a bone to pick with you, Grandma."

"Really? Would that be a *toe* bone?" She cackled.

How did she know about my faking a broken toe? Of course! Kathy! That sister of mine just couldn't keep her big mouth shut.

"What do you want, Jill? I'm busy."

"You're spying on Drake."

"Don't be ridiculous."

"Are you denying it?"

"Of course I am. Why would I spy on my tenant?"

"To check up on me, I imagine."

"Don't flatter yourself, girl. Do you think I spend all my time thinking about you?"

"Why else would you bug his flat?"

"I've already told you. I haven't bugged it."

"You're lying. I know you're lying. When I was in there recently, I saw your face on the TV screen."

"A figment of your imagination."

"And in the mirror."

"Had you been drinking?"

"No. I hadn't been drinking. It was definitely you. You're using magic of some kind to keep an eye on him in the privacy of his own flat. It's simply unacceptable. It's a blatant infringement of privacy."

"Blah, blah, blah, blah."

"Is that all you have to say about it?"

"What do you expect me to say? I have my reasons for keeping an eye on that *so-called* friend of yours."

"You can't spy on people like that."

"Want to bet?"

"I'll report you to The Bugle."

"I thought you hated that rag."

"I do, but if that's what it takes to stop you from spying on Drake, then I'll happily do it. I'm sure Dougal Bugle would love to run an article on your covert surveillance operation."

"I'm not worried about The Bugle or Dougal Whatshisface. He and I have an understanding."

"I don't care. I want you to stop. Right now!"

"If I do stop, I'll expect you to cover the cost of any damage done to my property."

"Drake isn't going to do any damage. He's a perfectly respectable businessman."

"Says you. But what do you really know about him?"

It was a good question. I didn't know very much about

Drake at all. I didn't know what line of business he was in. I didn't know any of his family or friends, other than Raven. But I wasn't about to tell Grandma that.

"Of course I know him, and I'd vouch for him every day of the week."

"On your head be it then."

"So you'll stop the surveillance?"

"Yes. Now, if you don't mind, I'm busy."

Chapter 24

It was the day of the Compass competition, and I was feeling really nervous. The fact that it was a team competition made it much worse. I hated the idea of letting my teammates down, and I certainly hated the idea of letting my *team captain* down. Lucy, Lester, the twins and their fiancés were all there to cheer us on. Before we went into the Range, I had a quick word with Grandma.

"Yes, what is it Jill? We don't have long. We need to get changed."

"I know I had a go at you about the surveillance thing, but I wanted to thank you for getting Jack Maxwell's transfer cancelled."

"What else was I supposed to do? I can't have one of my team members love-struck and distracted, can I?"

"I suppose not."

So that was why she'd done it. There was me thinking that she'd felt sorry for me because my love life was a mess, when in reality she'd just been worried about how it would affect the team. I should have known.

The Range had been kitted out with bleachers on three sides as it always was for competitions. On the fourth side, were the cubicles where we were to get changed. The other two members of North Team were waiting for us there.

"Jill, let me introduce you to your teammates," Grandma said. "This is Sophie Slater — she is a level four witch. This is Jasmine Jones — level five."

"Hi everyone. I feel like I'm letting the side down a bit name-wise. I'm the only one whose name isn't an alliteration: Sophie Slater, Jasmine Jones, Mirabel

Millbright, and then there's me, Jill Gooder."

"Can we focus on the competition, please?" Grandma tutted.

As with the Levels competition, we were required to wear traditional witch costume, which I did at least feel more comfortable in now. I slipped into the cubicle, got changed, and then re-joined my teammates.

I glanced across at the other teams: South, West, and East. The team captain of South Team was Ma Chivers. She saw me, and gave me a stony, cold look which froze me to the spot.

The first round of the competition was for the level three witches. The four of us stood on our own compass point around a large circle, which had been painted on the ground. The competitors were announced as: Jill Gooder, Lucy West, Coral Slade and Alex Xavier. All four of us were staring at the large boulder that had been placed in the centre of the circle.

On the judge's signal, we were to use the 'power' spell to try to push the boulder into the quadrant of one of the other witches. After thirty seconds, whichever witch had the boulder in their quadrant would be eliminated.

"Three — two — one — go."

It was immediately obvious that the other three witches were all trying to push the boulder into my quadrant. I wasn't sure whether they had agreed this tactic beforehand or if it was just coincidence; I suspected the former. Either way the odds were stacked against me. I had to somehow resist the force of three 'power' spells which was an almost impossible task. The boulder was already in my quadrant, and the clock was ticking.

I glanced across at my teammates. Sophie and Jasmine were shaking their heads. Grandma was staring at me, and it was as if I could read her thoughts: *Focus Jill, it's all about focus.*

But focus alone would not be enough, I had to have a strategy. I would never succeed if I tried to push straight ahead, but if I could deflect the boulder by focusing my force against just one of the other competitors — the one in the adjacent quadrant — I might yet survive.

There was a large clock to my left, and I could see the seconds counting down. Ten seconds to go, nine, eight. At the very last moment, I closed my eyes, and used every ounce of strength I had to deflect the boulder.

A bell rang — the round was over. I opened my eyes. The boulder had slid into the West quadrant. The announcer told the crowd that Alex Xavier, the witch from the West Team had been eliminated. I was through to round two.

In this round, we were given a task and had to decide for ourselves which was the most appropriate spell to use. A metal shield had been placed on a plinth in the centre of the circle. Our task was to raise the shield, and deliver it into our hands without damaging it in any way. We weren't allowed to move from our marks.

On the judge's signal, Lucy West was the first to react. She used the 'attract' spell, which sent the shield flying towards her. But she had very little control over it, and it flew past her, and crashed into the wall behind her, damaging the shield slightly. Lucy West was asked to step aside, and a new shield was placed on the plinth.

Coral Slade used the 'move' spell. It was notoriously

difficult to control objects over any distance with that spell, particularly if there was any weight involved. The shield was only halfway to her when she lost power, and it fell to the floor. Coral was asked to step aside, and a third shield was brought out.

It was my turn. I thought long and hard about which spell to use. I had to get it right. I cast the 'vortex' spell, and guided the mini tornado to the plinth. The force of the wind raised the shield, and then I guided it slowly back to me. When it was within touching distance, I grabbed the shield. The crowd erupted and I could see Aunt Lucy, Lester, and the twins cheering and shouting. They obviously thought I'd survived the round, and the judges confirmed that was the case when they eliminated Coral Slade.

I'd made it through to the third and final round. The plinth was removed, and in its place, a large metal pole was sunk deep into the ground. Tethered by a chain to the pole was a tiger. A circle was drawn around the pole to indicate how far the tiger's reach extended. One of the judges then threw a ring into the circle, which the tiger was now patrolling; it was getting angrier and angrier. Our task was to retrieve the ring.

I didn't react immediately upon the judge's signal. I thought it was more important to spend a moment considering which spell to use. After all, Grandma had emphasised that spell selection was everything. Lucy West, on the other hand, acted immediately by making herself invisible.

After a few seconds, the tiger seemed to become even more restless, and his attention was focused on one particular spot directly in front of him. He must have picked up Lucy's scent as she approached the circle. Then suddenly, the tiger struck out with its paw. The next moment, Lucy became visible again. She was holding her arm, and I could see spots of blood on her clothes. She'd obviously reached inside the circle to pick up the ring; the tiger had followed its nose and dealt her a painful blow. She didn't appear to be seriously injured, but it was bad enough to eliminate her from the tournament.

It was my turn. I walked slowly towards the circle, and when I was only a few yards away, I cast the 'obscurer' spell to create a smoke screen. The smoke was very thick and acrid. As I drew closer to the circle, I could just about make out the tiger. It was at the opposite side of the circle. It obviously didn't like the smell of the smoke. When I was close enough, I crouched down, grabbed the ring and backed away. I'd made it!

Once again, the crowd erupted, and the judges confirmed that I was the winner of the first round of the Compass competition. I glanced over at my teammates. Sophie and Jasmine were cheering and clapping. Grandma looked on impassively.

It was the next round of the competition; this time for level four witches. Our representative, Sophie Slater, was as nervous as a kitten. Jasmine and I did our best to calm her down. Grandma, in typical grandma fashion, told her to 'just get on with it'.

Nervous or not, Sophie sailed through the first eliminator, and just managed to scrape through the second. In the final round, she faced the level four witch from the East Team. This round was based on the 'jump' spell; a spell I positively hated. I was glad that I hadn't had to face it in my round. The competitors moved over to where two parallel walls were standing. Each of the walls had numerous ledges projecting from it, and on each ledge was a single gold coin. The competitors had to use the 'jump' spell to leap from wall to wall, landing on each ledge to collect the coins. The witch who ended up with the most coins would be declared the winner. Whoever had designed this had obviously played way too many video games.

Three — two — one — and they were off.

I could barely bring myself to watch. How they avoided one another when they were flying backwards and forwards between the two walls was beyond me. I kept expecting one of them to plunge to the ground.

I tried to keep count of how many coins Sophie had collected, but it all happened so quickly, it was impossible. Within little more than a minute, both witches had handed their haul to the judges. We all waited with bated breath until the announcement came.

'Here are the results: Sophie Slater, North Team, fourteen coins; Linda Bale, East Team, fifteen coins.'

Poor Sophie. She'd lost out by a single coin, and was absolutely devastated. Jasmine and I did our best to console her. Grandma said nothing.

It was time for the level five round. Sophie had managed to pull herself together enough to wish Jasmine luck. Jasmine sailed through the first two eliminators with no problem, and now faced Dawn Treemore from the South Team in the final round. I glanced across at Ma Chivers; just like Grandma, she was stony faced. Behind her, I spotted Alicia and Cyril.

This round was one of the most dangerous I'd ever witnessed. The two witches were to use the 'thunderbolt' spell to fire at a target which had been placed right next to their opponent. They each had to fire three thunderbolts.

I turned to Grandma. "This is crazy. Why don't they have the targets in a safe area rather than right next to the competitors?"

"It's a test not only of accuracy, but of nerve. It's one thing to fire a thunderbolt, but it's an entirely different matter to do it while your opponent's thunderbolts are landing all around you."

"Surely someone could get hurt?"

"It's unlikely, but it does happen occasionally. At least if it does, you have the consolation of knowing your opponent has missed the target."

Some consolation!

Three — two — one — go.

Dawn fired her first thunderbolt; it hit the outer of the three rings. Jasmine's first thunderbolt hit the second ring of the target.

Dawn fired again, and this time, she hit the bullseye.

Jasmine fired her second thunderbolt and also hit the bullseye.

Dawn fired again and scored another bullseye.

It was all down to the last thunderbolt. If Jasmine hit the bullseye, she would win. If she hit the second circle, it would be a tie and they would fire again. If she missed or hit the outer circle, she would lose.

You could have heard a pin drop.

Jasmine took a deep breath and fired. The thunderbolt hit the outer circle.

Despondent, Jasmine re-joined us. "Sorry guys. I guess I lost my nerve."

Sophie and I reassured her that she had done her best. Once again, Grandma said nothing.

It was now all down to the final round which was for the level six witches. If the West quadrant won the next round, the tournament would be a four-way tie, but if any of the other quadrants won, there would be an outright winner.

The witch from the West quadrant was eliminated first, so now we were sure to have an overall winner. The next witch to be eliminated was from the East quadrant which meant whoever won the final round would take the cup. The two level six witches remaining were Grandma and Ma Chivers. This was a rerun of the final of the Elite competition, which had ended in stalemate, much to Grandma's annoyance. The spell to be used was also the same one as in the Elite competition. The difference this time was there was no time limit; there had to be a winner.

As we were waiting for them to start, my mind went back to my recent visit to Grandma's house. When I'd seen her in her bedroom, she'd seemed so vulnerable, and annoyed at herself because her magic had failed her. Was she losing her power? Would she be able to withstand the might of Ma Chivers, or would she fold under pressure? The tension in the stadium was almost unbearable.

Three — two — one.

The two powerful witches locked minds just as they had in the Elite competition. The stress on both women's faces was evident. One moment Grandma seemed to have the upper-hand, the next moment, Ma Chivers looked to be in control. I was terrified that Grandma would crack under the pressure. I didn't mind if we lost the tournament; it was the long-term effect on Grandma that worried me. Losing to Ma Chivers was not something that she would get over easily.

Then, out of nowhere, Ma Chivers stumbled and slumped to the floor. Grandma had won! She'd overcome her! The crowd erupted. Sophie, Jasmine and me rushed over to Grandma.

"Don't make such a fuss." She brushed us aside.

I glanced over at Ma Chivers who was stumbling to her feet. She was obviously okay, but a little stunned, and more than a little annoyed.

Aunt Lucy and the twins joined us down on the playing field to congratulate Grandma. We'd won the Compass competition! Grandma had once again proven herself to be the most powerful witch in Candlefield. Perhaps I need no longer worry about what I'd witnessed at her house that day. Maybe it had been no more than a blip. Today was Grandma's day. Today she had led her team to victory in the Compass competition for the third year in a row.

And it felt good.

Chapter 25

I thought Jack might have called me by now to arrange a date, but I hadn't heard a word from him since he'd told me that his transfer had been cancelled. I'd tried to call him on his mobile a couple of times—just to check he was okay, but he hadn't picked up. I'd left voicemails, but he hadn't returned them. Maybe he was ill. Or maybe he was being an idiot. Either way, I needed to know what was going on.

I decided to call the main desk at the police station to see if I could get through to him that way.

"Hello, Washbridge Police," a tired and bored voice said.

"Hi, there. My name is Jill Gooder. Could I speak to Jack Maxwell, please?"

"Sorry, that's not possible."

"Is he in?"

"Like I said, it's not possible to speak to Detective Maxwell at the moment."

"Do you know when he'll be in?"

"Like I said, it's not possible to speak to Detective Maxwell at the moment."

I was getting nowhere fast, so I hung up. Was he trying to avoid me? It certainly seemed that way, and yet after his transfer had been cancelled, I thought we'd really made a connection for the first time. I'd thought this was a new beginning for us. Had I got it wrong? Again?

If he *was* messing me about, I at least deserved to know, so I decided to go to the police station to confront him. It was easy to ignore a ringing phone, but it would be much more difficult to ignore me if I was in his face.

When I walked into the main reception area, there was a queue a mile long. Great! Oh, well. There was nothing to do but wait. I could just about handle the queue and the wait, but I couldn't handle the idiot who was standing in front of me. Not only did he have more mouth than brains, but he also had bad breath. And, he insisted on turning around every few minutes to tell me why he was there, how the police were incompetent, and what he would do if he was in charge. None of which made a lick of sense.

In the end, I couldn't stand it any longer. There were a few chairs at the side of the room. I pulled one of them over, and the next time he turned around, I cast the 'sleep' spell. He slumped quietly and peacefully onto the chair.

It was forty minutes before I eventually made it to the front of the queue. The police officer, who had a red nose and sunken eyes, lifted his head.

"Yes, how can I help you, madam?"

"My name is Jill Gooder, and I'm here to see Detective Maxwell."

"He's not available."

"What do you mean, '*not available*'? Is he in?"

"Detective Maxwell is not available."

"Where is he?"

"He isn't here."

"But where is he?"

"Not here."

The conversation went back and forth for a good five minutes, but I was no further forward. Something wasn't right. There was more to this than just Jack ignoring me. Where could he be? Why did they keep saying he wasn't there? I had to find out what was going on.

I stepped outside the police station, found a quiet doorway, made myself invisible, and then followed someone back inside the building. It was easy for me to slip over the desk without being noticed. I'd been in the police station several times before, and knew my way around. When I reached Jack Maxwell's office, it was empty, so I made my way to the conference rooms. There were two men in the first one, and I could overhear their conversation.

"Who's going to be leading the investigation now that Maxwell's been thrown off the case?" one of them said.

Thrown off the case? Not *taken* off the case, or *moved* to another case. That didn't sound good.

"It's ridiculous," the second man said. "The idea that Jack would take a bribe is just too daft for words."

"No smoke without fire."

"Shut up, Arthur. Jack Maxwell is as honest as the day is long. This is a setup. Somebody has screwed him over right and proper."

I could hardly believe my ears. No wonder they'd been so cagey when I tried to contact Jack by phone, and then again at the desk. It sounded as though he'd been suspended on suspicion of taking a bribe. Jack Maxwell might have his faults; I knew that better than most, but there was no way that he would ever take a bribe. Somebody had definitely set him up. I had to find Jack. Maybe I could help him?

If he'd let me.

After what felt like a thousand phone calls to his mobile, and almost as many voicemails, Jack Maxwell eventually called me back.

"Jill, have you been trying to contact me?"

"Only all day. I must have called you a thousand times."

"Sorry, I switched my phone off."

He sounded remarkably calm under the circumstances.

"Where are you?"

"I'm in a bar. The Sheep Shank on Evil Street, do you know it?"

"Yeah. I'm coming over now."

I made my way over to Evil Street, and found him sitting at the bar with another man.

"This is my second in command, Tom Hawk. Tom, this is Jill Gooder, the private investigator I told you about."

"So, you're the infamous Jill Gooder, are you?" Tom Hawk grinned. "I've heard a lot about you."

"All bad I imagine?"

"Most of it." He laughed.

"Look, I'd better get going," Tom said. "I'll catch up with you later, Jack."

"Okay. See you later."

"I hear you've been suspended," I said, as soon as we were on our own.

He looked surprised. "How did you find out?"

"It doesn't matter."

"No doubt from that inside source of yours?"

"We've had this conversation before. I don't have an 'inside source'."

"So, how do you know? It's not common knowledge."

"I'm a P.I. It's what I do. Anyway, never mind how I found out. What have they accused you of?"

"Look, I don't really want to discuss it."

"Come on, Jack. What's going on? Why have they

suspended you?"

"If you must know, they found money in the boot of my car. A lot of money."

"That's ridiculous! Even if you were on the take, you'd hardly leave the cash in the boot of your car."

"Obviously I wouldn't. Someone planted it there."

"So, why suspend you? Surely your bosses must realise you've been set up?"

"I'm sure they do, but they have to follow protocol. You know what it's like; everything has to be done by the book. The first step is to suspend me, then they'll bring in internal affairs. Once that happens, it'll all be cleared up pretty quickly, and I'll be back at work."

"I admire your blind faith in the system."

"What else can I do?"

"Why don't you let me help?"

"Definitely not! I don't want you sticking your oar in. Internal affairs will sort this out in no time; I'll be back at work in a matter of days. A week or two at the most. Whereas if you get involved — heaven knows what might happen."

"Thank you for that vote of confidence."

"I mean it, Jill. I don't want you getting involved. Promise me you won't."

"But—"

"Promise!"

"Okay, okay. I promise."

Liar, liar, pants on fire.

***

"Why the long face, lady?" Winky jumped onto my

desk.

"No reason."

"Come on. You can tell your uncle Winky. You know I'm a good listener."

"If you must know, Jack Maxwell has been suspended. Those idiots he works for have accused him of taking a bribe. Just when I thought he and I had a clear run, this gets in the way."

"Jack Maxwell, eh? Problems with his job, eh? You see. Madam Winkesca really *can* see into the future." He grinned that stupid grin of his. "Hey, what are you doing with that stapler? Put it down! Don't you dare throw that—"

Drat! Missed him again.

ALSO BY ADELE ABBOTT

The Witch P.I. Mysteries:

The Susan Hall Mysteries:

Whoops! Our New Flatmate Is A Human.
Whoops! All The Money Went Missing.
Whoops! There's A Canary In My Coffee
See web site for availability.

AUTHOR'S WEB SITE
http:www.AdeleAbbott.com

FACEBOOK
http://www.facebook.com/AdeleAbbottAuthor

MAILING LIST
(new release notifications only)
http:/AdeleAbbott.com/adele/new-releases/

54696603R00129

Made in the USA
Columbia, SC
04 April 2019